[Ex]tinguished & [Ex]tinct:
An Anthology of Things That No Longer Exist

[EX]TINGUISHED & [EX]TINCT

An Anthology of Things That No Longer Exist

~

Edited by John McCarthy

Twelve Winters Press
Sherman, Illinois

Published by
Twelve Winters Press, LLC

P. O. Box 414
Sherman, IL 62684-0414

TwelveWinters.com

[Ex]tinguished & [Ex]tinct: An Anthology of Things That No Longer Exist,
was first published by Twelve Winters Press in 2014.

Editor: John McCarthy
Associate Editor: Pamm Collebrusco
Cover & Interior Page Design: John McCarthy
Cover Photo: "Tasmanian Tiger" copyright © Joanna Barnum

ISBN

978-0-9895151-4-6

Printed in the United States of America

Table of Contents

Prose Poetry

Prose

Ω

Editor's Preface

The writer's job is to represent a voice, not just an individualized, nuanced voice but a voice of collective import, a voice that speaks to and for a wider consciousness, regardless of brevity or permanence. With the weight of that voice, clearly defined objectives should present themselves. A new image should emerge. Perception should change, or at least become reinforced in the positive.

The theme for this anthology evolved—appropriately—from a conversation about the way writers seek to preserve all things, concrete and abstract. The present is fleeting faster than our nerve endings and synapses can capture and relate it through some form of simulacrum. As a result, it seemed unnecessary and fruitless to produce another contemporary anthology for quick consumption. The theory behind this anthology seemed to ask for something that begged for awareness.

There were too many things—animals, plants, electronic devices, etc.—that are no longer around because attempts to preserve them have failed, or they are quickly becoming extinct as a failure to preserve them. Necessity seemed like a fitting word to inscribe to the existence, or non-existence, of these things. And as writers, if preservation of the present is a common goal, then giving a collective voice to things past seemed like an obligation. Preservation as concern means we must revisit things that no longer exist and give them another chance, another voice. Bringing awareness to what their essence once was simply allows us to see more, beyond the limits of ourselves in the present.

Time is an interesting concept in that regard. Humans tend to perceive it as linear, point to ever distant point. But time is not a line if it is to be understood in its fullest sense. It is circular, and if you want to start getting esoteric and eschatological, time may not even exist at all. With this belief, all things that are now considered extinct—as the title of this anthology suggests—may not be extinct at all. The contents of this anthology are a step toward that mode of thought, that all things past, present, and future are in union, not separated by illusory construct. Voices and the printed page can transcend time with a will to believe and acknowledgment that they still exist in some kind of universal time.

Animals are just one item tied to the definition of extinction. A few pieces in this anthology deal with family relations and concrete objects that are no longer used in modern, everyday life, but have a place in nostalgia and memory. Feelings can threaten the existence of a relationship. Advancement in technology leads to the cannibalization of itself. It is a cycle and all of time is a recycling of itself. Nostalgia and memory exist in the present and future. The pieces within, chosen from a plethora of great submissions, help propel this cycle of realization that all things considered to no longer exist, in fact do.

All extinction replaces itself with a new kind of life. Extinction is a materialistic belief. All things still exist in some way, be it words on a page or in our consciousness. Let us not forget that. A more appropriate subtitle for this anthology would be things that no longer exist in the traditional sense of existence. Once something is, it is eternal. This anthology is a manifestation of that belief.

I would also like to acknowledge for their hard work and collaboration in helping to edit this anthology Pamm Collebrusco and Ted Morrissey. Thanks to them, and thanks to you, the reader.

John McCarthy

February 1, 2014
Springfield, Illinois

John McCarthy's work has appeared, or is forthcoming in, *The Pinch*, *Salamander*, *Oyez Review*, *Midwestern Gothic*, *Jabberwock Review*, *SPECS*, *The Conium Review*, *Digital Americana*, and *The Lindenwood Review*, among others. He lives in Springfield, Illinois, where he is a contributing editor at *Poets' Quarterly* and the assistant editor of *Quiddity* International Literary Journal and Public-Radio Program.

Ezra Olson

Selections[†]

For A. R. Wallace

We will now discuss in a little more detail the struggle for existence
—Charles Darwin, *The Origin of Species*

I.

I am aware it is doubtful what forms are
                admitted, perfected, beautiful—
woodpecker and mistletoe, parasite
or bird, the structure of which dives
                in the breeze. Everywhere, every world.
        And I produce through knowledge
nothing in words

of nature, dimly seen, which round us—songsters,
                eggs, nestlings—though superabundant
        is not all recurring. I should premise:
I, being and including life,
                may be said to live. The edge of life,
        though, can sense, devour, increase
its animal.

Cannot, would not…? No. The earth has doubled and
                in a few years I will be old. But
        this is quite incredible. In new homes
we and I forget and produce
                and produce, and the ostrich is to
        fly, but how can a life be
destroyed, extinct?

The tree lived, a seed ensured in looking at
                its life. Each face I recall, suffer.
        This which I have made I suffer also,

ground cleared where I grow, though grown, grow.
                    With the elephant, birds, animals,
            often we even appear
parasitic.

And our fields, barren, with two or three birds, see
                    the enclosed hill-tops, years, spaces, close.
            I could not see but looking closely I
counted and tried and failed and searched,
                    wild, and in feral and increasing
            circles of battle and so
in ignorance.

I am one bound by a web of occasion.
                    In England, I tried to reach nectar.
            In England, humble-bees destroy their combs.
All over England, I have found
                    the average checks. And, entangled, we
            chance a view of surrounding
forests, trees, seeds:

Insect and insect; insects, snails, birds and beasts
                    and trees and a handful of feathers
            and a parasite—they will generally
disappear. They cannot be kept.
                    Habits though, habits and, and structure—
            They, we see, swallow the song
of the cockroach.

Forms nearly victorious may be deduced.
                    And the diving escape seems to have
            a power over the confines that may
be exactly the same as its
                    imagination. Form, convince us
            of ignorance. We console
ourselves with fear.

II.

I, it is admitted, structure the breeze

through words, which, though recurring, may devour

the earth. But this is incredible. We—

I—forget the ostrich, the tree, a face.

Recall this ground where we appear, and see

the enclosed years. I counted in circles

and tried to destroy their England. I found,

entangled, we view birds and feathers and

disappear, though we swallow song forms and—

diving—escape the confines of ourselves.

III.

Words appear; and ~~years,~~
~~circles, and I,~~ we, ~~birds and~~
~~feathers~~ disappear.

---

†Part I is an erasure of Charles Darwin's *The Origin of Species*, specifically chapter three, on the "Struggle for Existence." Part II is an erasure of Part I, and Part III is an erasure of Part II. The words and their order are Darwin's; their selection, punctuation, and occasional capitalization are the author's.

Lynn Pedersen

Something about Darwin

Most of earth's animals have become extinct: moas, mammoths,
ammonites, mastodons, saber-toothed cats. If anyone

should understand such loss it's Darwin—
cartographer of tails and limbs. Permian

to Triassic. Mesozoic to Cenozoic. Epochs and eras.
But this is abstraction, like political boundaries on a map

or saying Monday bleeds into Tuesday
and Monday is gone (gone where?),

and what happened to Monday's sound, its light?

What's tangible is the space left:
fossil footprints, my fingers fit the grooves

of Cambrian seas, rocky joists, my knuckles
dovetail Jurassic backbones.

But there is no account in the Origin of Species
of grief. No Cretaceous eulogy. No prediction that 300 million years

after the trilobites I should mourn the loss of any of these.
Is it only tragic when the last

of a species dies? How about the first born? The ones sited in the middle
in strata of rock or ancient sands?

Where have they gone? Who grieves for them?

Lynn Pedersen

A Brief History of the Passenger Pigeon

Not to be confused with messenger pigeons, birds sent behind enemy lines in war, but think passengers as in birds carrying suitcases, sharing a berth on a train, or traveling in bamboo cages on a ship, always migrating on a one-way to extinction. How would extinction look on a graph? A steady climb, or a plateau with a precipitous cliff at the dawn of humans?

Nesting grounds eight hundred square miles in area. Skies swollen with darkening multitudes. Days and days of unbroken flocks passing over. *Ectopistes migratorius*.

And the last of the species, Martha, named for Martha Washington, dies in a cage in 1914 at the Cincinnati Zoo.

Forget clemency. We are the worst kind of predator, not even deliberate in our destruction. Our killing happens à la carte, on the side (side of Dodo?).

And because the nineteenth century did not enlist a battlefield artist for extinctions, there are no official witnesses to the slaughter, just participants. If you could somehow travel back to this scene, through the would-be canvas, you would run flailing your arms toward the hardwood forests and the men with sticks and guns and boiling sulphur pots to bring birds out of the trees, as if you could deliver 50,000 individual warnings, or throw yourself prostrate on the ground, as if your one body could hold sway.

Daniel Hudon

Recalling the Golden Toad, Now Extinct[†]

Like a dream conjured by the pools of the cloud forest, longing for a splash of color amid the monotony of rot and decay far below the canopy. The pools themselves fleeting, brought by the mists that creep over the mountains of Monteverde, the spring rains. Neon Day-glo orange males, eyes like round black jewels, thought to be deaf and dumb, sensing by vibration, summoned from underground by the life-giving pools. And for a few weeks the pools would thrive in the mating frenzy when the olive-colored females arrived. This went on once a year for a long time. The pools still awaken but can no longer summon the toads. Some dreams only come true once. On a night hike, our flashlight beams shine into the clouds like searchlights in the cosmic dark.

[†]Last seen in 1989. Extinction possibly due to climate change, El Niño (which caused the pools to dry up early) and the chytrid fungus, which is decimating amphibians worldwide.

Daniel Hudon

The Laysan Rail[†]
—*Porzana Palmeri*

Flightless and fearless, the sandy-brown Laysan rail was swift and curious. It darted over the sand from one patch of grass to another or crept gingerly through the grass, poking its head forward and from side to side inquisitively, and it was often seen stopped in the shade of a plant peering at an object with one foot poised in air before advancing again in fits and starts. In spring, their fuzzy-black chicks scuttled about under the parents, venting surprising amounts of noise.

In the only video of the Laysan rail, shot in 1923, one scrambles from the bottom to the top of the frame with its head down, taking long, sure strides across the sand between a pair of coral outcroppings; an instant later, another dashes after it and for a moment it looks like a repeat of the same bird, running the same way. But then you see, just as the bird leaves the top of the frame, it flaps its short wings, once, twice, in an effort to catch its mate. If you loop this short clip, the chase goes on forever.

[†] Extinction due to introduced rabbits, which denuded the island, wiping out the bird's vegetative protection and the moths and insects, such as the brine fly, it depended on. Last seen in 1923.

Daniel Hudon

The Carolina Parakeet: The Great Disappearing Act[†]
—Conuropsis carolinensis

On cold winter days while snow covered the land, a streak of green would alight from the sky and descend upon the barren branches of a large sycamore tree. When the sun shone brightly upon the inhabited tree top, the many yellow heads looked like so many candles, like a kind of Christmas tree.

*

One of the tragic habits of the Carolina parakeet was for the flock to sweep repeatedly around a wounded or dead companion squawking and screeching until they too fell to the hunter.

*

In midsummer, with the tree fully leafed out, flying with such a boisterous din, the birds would all pitch into the tree and become silent. So great had been the din just a second before and now, green within green, they disappeared into the tree, leaving a bewildering stillness.

[†] Extinction due to over-hunting. The last Carolina parakeet died in 1914.

Daniel Hudon

Urania Sloanus at Sunrise[†]

When the pear tree blossoms, one after another begins to appear just as the sun rises—*whence they come is a mystery*—and their velvet black wings, banded in metallic blue-green and flecked with red and gold, now radiate ever more brilliantly as the sunbeams glint off them, and, fluttering, by dozens, by hundreds, dizzy with the fragrance of the bloom, the glancing light sparkling from myriad refractions so bright one must almost shield the eyes, they engage in playful combats, dancing in their joyousness, crazy with delight, wheeling and soaring higher and higher above the tree, flying up and up till they are lost to sight.

[†] Sometimes called the most beautiful moth in the world, *Urania Sloanus* was last seen in 1894 or 1895 in Jamaica. Extinction due to habitat loss and loss of one of its larval food plants. The quote is from Lady Edith Blake and the piece is based on descriptions by her and Philip Henry Gosse.

Daniel Hudon

The Extinction of the Falkland Islands Wolf:
A Tragedy in Five Parts

Act I

The Falkland Islands wolf (*Dusicyon australis*) takes advantage of low sea levels during the last ice age and a narrow frozen marine strait to colonize the Falkland Islands, where it lives unmolested by other predators for thousands of years. It builds burrows and feeds on sea birds.

Act II

The wolf is discovered by Captain John Strong when he lands on the islands in 1690. He compares it to a fox that is "twice as big as those in England." Seventy-five years later, in 1765, the wolf's curiosity is revealed when four of them run belly-deep into the sea to welcome a landing party from Commodore Byron of the HMS Dolphin. The sailors mistake the wolf's tame exuberance for ferocity and, unarmed, pull back to the ship.

Act III

When Charles Darwin visits the islands on the Beagle in 1833-34, gauchos tell him they frequently kill the wolf by tempting it with a chunk of meat in one hand and then stabbing it with the other. Darwin describes the wolf's fearlessness: "They have been observed to enter a tent and actually pull some meat from beneath the head of a sleeping seaman."

He also sees the writing on the wall for the wolf and writes: "Within a few years after these islands have become settled, in all probability this fox [wolf] will be classed as with the dodo, as an animal which has perished from the face of the earth."

Act IV

Not long after Darwin's departure, the colonial government sets bounty on the animals. Hunters sent by fur dealer John Jacob Astor of New York beginning around 1839 fill his store with so many pelts the wolf is nearly extirpated.

Act V

The wolf is further demonized by Scottish settlers, arriving in the 1860s, for preying on cattle and sheep. Farmers lace dead geese with strychnine and place them in the wolves' burrows. Tales of wolves biting sheep in the neck lead to stories of vampires and the bounty is raised. The Falkland Islands wolf enters the annals of extinction as the first canid to become extinct in modern times when the last one is shot in 1876.

Majnun Ben-David

A County Without Weather

He was the only one who remembered when the county still had weather, he told himself with the satisfied certainty found only in the very young, very old, or very drunk. He possessed one of those attributes and was en route to adding a second as he leaned back in his chair, whiskey bottle in hand, and surveyed with approval the uniform green blur of his lawn. Lack of weather had been a blessing for the grass, no more browning summer heat or killing winter snows, no excuse now for having anything less than a solid carpet of bluegrass or, if you were that sort, fescue.

He remembered how it had been. The August heat like a rooftop sniper, people darting from a patch of shade into the redoubt of an air-conditioned store, nobody lingering in the open. The autumn leaves a quilt of colors, slick underfoot in the mist. The winter snow clogging the streets, a cold torpor slowing everything from the town firetruck to the small muscles in your hand.

The hell anybody here knew about that now. No seasons, no rain, no wind, no temperature. Thermometer mercury stayed in the bulb. Digital sensors blinked horizontal lines. His nephew, the one half-sensible member of his quarrelsome progeny, had checked the internet for him only to report that the county weather records were missing. Information no longer available, it said.

The weather hadn't gone away all at once, he remembered that. In the beginning people talked about it, greetings mixed with comments about the not-so-hot summer or hardly cold winter. The first megastore had just come in and it still stocked seasonal items, the plastic kiddie pools of summer and rickety sleds of winter. By the time the second megastore sprouted—out on Milt's old field, made the lucky bastard rich—it was the same merchandise year-round, or so one of his idiot sons-in-law told him.

Soon there was nothing you could say about the weather because there wasn't any. Instead you made small talk about the stores, the sales, and the boom. And what a boom it was, the big stores coming in, then their distribution centers, all on account, according to a fellow at the legion bar, of the county having a high uniformity rating. The stores, that's where the jobs were now. Outdoor work, like his forty years as an agricultural inspector, was dinosaur extinct.

To hell with all that, he thought for no real reason other than a fondness for the phrase. To hell with all that, he repeated, this time aloud. Then more whiskey.

A passing jogger found him the next morning in the yard, a lone sprinkler raining water down on his slack body and splashing off his black winter jacket, his thick hat and earmuffs askew, the lawn around him slick and muddy, his grin lopsided and toothless as he stared up blankly at the water pelleting down from the sky.

Susan Cohen

We Descend

The guide lifts his lantern:
A mare, her mane and
sloping muzzle thick black.

Her straight spine
holds against the sway
of a belly round with foal.

She is a pinto.
Someone painted her
with charcoal, ochre, fat

and spit. Someone breathing
this fungal air and lit by fire
in the Stone Age drew

a wakeful fish who swims
across the limestone
when the lantern swings.

We have invented nothing,
Picasso cried, emerging
from a cave like this.

They left palm prints,
their fingers splayed
as if waiting to be counted.

We resist the urge
to place our astonished
hands on theirs.

Susan Cohen

Rossio Square[†]

If I were any kind of real Jew
I'd recite *Kaddish* in this Lisbon square
where the National Theater rose
from the Hall of the Inquisition
and replaced the theater of auto-da-fe,
where final *Sh'mas* earned
the frenzied applause of flames.
But I am one of those Jews who,
without force or punishment,
has let go of most things Jewish
including Hebrew prayers,
and because I am that kind of Jew,
I stop amid the innocent tumult
of tourists and trams—
old smoke in the Portuguese air,
old grief wedged like grit
between the mosaic tiles patterned
like waves—a Jew struck still
by such combustion of souls.

[†]Rossio Square was the site of one of the bonfires during mass burnings in
April 1506 of 2,000 to 4,000 New Christians—Jews who were forcibly bap-
tized nine years earlier, many on the same site.

M.E. Silverman

The Last Jew
for Zablon Simintov, the last Jew of Afghanistan

I.

Sometimes we all feel like the last,
a single stick in a rushing river.
Honestly, who has not felt
hairs rise on the base of their neck
when hands cup to other ears
full of distressing whispers? Listen:

today you are the Last Jew.

You could be in Calcutta or Krakow,
any place given to time
for those *olim* who made *aliyah*.
"Next year in Jerusalem"
they said dutifully
until they did.

Today you are the Last

Jew, the chosen carpet dealer
in the heart of Kabul
where Hebrew letters breathe
like morning birds,
where echoes sink in surrounding streets,
unswept rooms & broken glass,
an eerie emptiness,
a staleness under cracked fans
& dusty cupboards
of books, hundreds
of years old, where God
grumbles to you & you alone.

Every Friday night,
the missing make a slight noise
that sounds like leaves,
sounds like sand,
like wings passing
by, flutters in the sky.

Do you hoist the Torah
above your shoulders, bear it
around the sanctuary for ghosts
to touch it with their *tallises*?

On the Sabbath, do you kiss
the book? Recite the prayers?
Who do you preach to? Who
in your synagogue is teaching?

"I don't know why I'm still
living here." To anyone
who cares, you say
the reason you stay, avoid
seeing your wife for over a decade
& your two Zionist children
is "God's will," but when
Moses confronted the pharaoh
or when Abraham left his home in Ur,
God never instructed them to become
like locust living off what the land offers,
to abandon their family.

So you watch, you wait—
we wonder. Today

you are the Last Jew.

II.

In the Jerusalem Wing

the Tree of Life is empty.
This is no mistake.

Please believe.
This keeps Zablon awake at night,

how they'd coat it with iron,
store it in a corner wing

the color of slate.
No cameras to record

the scene. Not even a guard.
Here in the Natural History Museum

in a section reserved
for the dioramas of the forgotten

one can take the tour

to see it
in the southwest corner.

For a fee.

III.

The Last Jew will be born sometime
                    after
                        you read this,

with matzah colored skin
                    & Talmudic
                    eyes,

            with the breath
                    of a lost language
                    that speaks

to salt & ash,

begins
　　　　with *baruch*,
　　　　beginning of a prayer,
　　　　　　which most ignore

like the bearded veteran
　　　　who holds a sign
　　　　which could be a board
　　　　　　from the ark

on the corner
　　　　of Main
　　　　& 10th.
　　　　　　For a few,

it will feel familiar
　　　　like the moment
　　　　right before

a sneeze
　　　　& the bless
you, a fraction
of a second

where you know
　　　　what will come next,
　　　　& then

it is
gone.

M.E. Silverman

Noah Knows No Evil

At first, he didn't want the birds,
fearing the crows, the ravens,
really all the blackbirds,
their night-glow eyes,
those devilish heads that twitch,
switching side to side, always ready,

always hungry. In truth,
he believed any creature evil who can
simply stretch away,
sway with the winds
and break through plumes,
who can flutter & rush in an instant

from rising waters & rain.
He never, not once, would watch
them flap their wing
& fly from this dark earth
by gliding their frail bodies
into the open heavens' blue arc.

M.E. Silverman

The Last Jew's Wife

The day I wished her gone I saw the table where we sit,
empty, near the two water marks & the huge blot,
the burnt circle in the middle made by your first stew,
stained black with splotches of rust-like brown
from first anniversary or first job or maybe first check,
when a good meal meant music & laughter
& sex, but now the middle is worn by weight, by years
of plates & fat pots, by heat & blemishes
from meat & pasta & god-knows-what,
the endless scraping, the scratches, the splinters,
corners chipped & rubbed soft, the time spent polishing
with the turpentine mixed with two ounces of beeswax
to bring the luster back, the history of a family,
forgotten moments gone like the woman
who wished to be as visible
as this table.

Elmaz Abinader

Lines of Demarcation
after Alexander Fernandez, Architect

I.

Alejandro says truth is immediate if you rest
a sketch book on your lap and make a line—

drawing without direction loosens hinges
undoes beginnings and endings

size and form   and everything
is petal or fern, its own infinity

Witness a drawing's wisdom—kindle
what must be rendered or left behind. Collect
geography on the distal phalanx, rub it over your lips

to speak not of permanence but the fluidity where
inhabitation composts a new geology.

II.

Wind is the pen   sea the chisel: granite, slate
striated elders' eyelids long   cliff inscribed
benedictions washed into their faces—

even the mountains burst through the earth
volcanic explosions   calm to sea—
wait, another battering comes from the wind,
north and south, unkindness moves

into confusion, a murder of skin
a flattening of the head, the curve

of the shoulder, an anatomy carved by desires
terrain re-formed

animals show up dead   misguided after years
of knowing their own place and people
of traveling along the prescribed and certain routes
of hieroglyphs of paw prints, oases dried (en)danger ahead.

III.

Anticipate the crush, the metal deposition
of this earth, the rumbling, the lifting up
sod under the hooves of the elk moose pronghorns—
the bellowing song surfacing cylindrical drums
rolling down to the river and floating.

Snow fragments the larger elements:
chimney through roof, trunk extending
below branches—bark more pronounced
brick more emphatic, supple.

Boot prints carve the pure field
leading not to the house but deeper
into the wood, more confounded
by the wisdom of silence.

The storm goes on:
inside the chest, catapulting
the particles that have been sweetly
secured now unearthed.

IV.

I'll ride the tectonic landmass   visit the lost ones
speak their language borrow their breath
sign their names to books read unread

I peel the skin   shave the crust away

leave membrane   bones unconstructed.

The absence of color is where my body
touches space where I carve from the sky
an outline of my posture planted
my position   moving headlong

Bring the quiet of the night into the day
a map   of days, of years, of ages
            like so many things

V.

Footprints numberline the path   wash of tide
the shore anticipates the sea comes toward it
casts a story   a chalk line filled with mercury memory

arrowhead rain slams glass or so I think
this storm is a dream or the insistence
of epochs entering my sleep so   I waken worrying

I have lived under the house
just off the stone road
where the soldiers stripped the pictures
from the wall, spray painted
limestone slurs against

the vacant residents underdressed
hover in strange territories, feel
their bodies to find familiarity
hot whispers   a language unrecognized

VI.

She joined him as many do, traded lineage
for frontier, for children born away from situ
and sacrament. Dirt hard on the shoe
soles cracked to western sun. This is her midnight—

no one said life might be alone

She becomes hardwood planted in a slosh of soil
not able to hold the weight of her tide. Not native here
or anywhere. When the children are born
tendrils braid into new systems.

Reverse the stroke, comfort the hand that soothed,
un-grip the fist to make a leaf, veins like string,
soften trees to skin, of check, of chin, of heel.

Give timbre to the voices, silken the threads knitted
into the nest among the twigs. She hums a lullaby,
not for sleep or silence, memory

sprouting from an unseen root   too deep
in the soil to identify. She stays where she is left
lacing vines of ache hunger

VII.

Life in order is captive,
susceptible to systems. Slivers of madness
are fitted between air and object,
artery and blood.

The storm is the windfall
of grace sufficient to explain
the anxiety of our own selves as strangers
to this landscape.

So every day the power to transform
relies upon time and erosions,
storms and fires, imminent transfusion

earths' blood altered, channeling the story
that was west, east, the nothing to the
something left to translate and remember—

puzzle this earth, locate the pieces of tundra
of desert, palm and alder,
to read that moment like no other.

VIII.

This trumpet this timpani beats
in the heart of the earth, injects
a warmth in the dead of an isolated
winter. Not only as an explanation
for the mountains but as a witness to them.
We cannot stop the eruptions, each chord
Incandescent/dissonant

This may be the revelation
we wait for: that everything we
want to know, remember, treasure
holds up in our fingers hungry for, recognition:
Uncurl the fist, hold the pencil
put memory to the task.

It will skate away from you unbound
paper boat on water, particle of flower
airborne. What escapes is written elsewhere.

Elmaz Abinader

Ash Wednesday

Our skin is under contract, and in the end, this crisp cloak returns to the earth.
I measure the weight of my granules, feel the shifting toward death along
my neckline crossing my chest looping rib and vertebrate.

My heart beats a ripple across the skin, the lungs inflate/deflate
softened by fine hairs and scented oils, nerve fibers violining a restless music
down my legs mounting joints and skiing shins, ankles and feet

I feel in its dust the desert composition—canyon and mesa—
alive and dead at the same time

This dust: infinity sheds its cells, the surface   fuses elements
dermis, pores, corneum; scars a silhouette of bodies gone—
here at the end of my fingertips shivers a cold anxiousness
reluctant absolution

And what does this make me?
Element upon element, mineral mixed with platelets and papillae—
Am I a mountaintop above tree line pulling my roots toward nourishment
or an arroyo sunk into the abdomen, the sedimentary pelvis of the desert?
How do I stir my earth into life?

Elmaz Abinader

In the Throat I

It was an old theme even for me: Language cannot do everything.
—Adrienne Rich, *Cartographies of Silence*

if I could speak
the hyphen making space between the word and what it needs

then I could learn how this body can inhabit two worlds—a cable surging
power from one land to the next

I could verbalize
delicacy of reference, elbow the comma to clarify, that I am not recent
but a long time resident holding a steady job, not belonging to unworthy society

simplified
by the colon that actualizes my history to be concurrent with yours
despite my name that could be translated, not to the same tongue

perhaps explain
that many things are true; that I am connected without conjunction
and the woman with my face died with all our names woven under her hair.

Elmaz Abinader

Heartwood†

While you watch   you are being watched
and every word you write   is scribed on arm   henna
petrified with the veins of your witnessing.

You need to grow harder than fresh limbs
slick and sentient reaching and waiting.
Solidify the cambium harden your bark
capture your tears inside of your trunk,
molten tributaries moving with life—

What is seen are grandmothers
skimming barbed-wire
stuffing groceries under their skirts   scrambling over the gate
as you tick off one after another up and over   your jeep idles near the wall

The pinch of the wire just refreshes old scars
they don't think as much of it as you do when

your organs soak with sugars
all the blood is trapped below
your heart. Even while it chokes you

the cells confine the color
drained from your face

as you watched them escape
to the other side of the same square of dust,   crippled tired
pulling on a power of healed-over wounds as thick as branches.

Examine those albino eyes
expressionless stupefyingly blind
and see in them rings of endless years
of stunted growth, roots lengthening below the terrain.

Where the heart-wood thickens,   they have power
no one can see into the tree
where everything dead gathers and protects them
        stone core wood heart.

† As a tree grows, older xylem cells in the center of the tree become inactive
and die, forming heartwood. Because it is filled with stored sugar, dyes and
oils, the heartwood is usually darker than the sapwood. The main function of
the heartwood is to support the tree.

Christina Lovin

Elms

In memory of the Lombard Elm, 1868-1965

I.

Elms graced the white-lined streets of town
like timeworn widows or those old maids found
at any church potluck at Lincoln Park—elegant
but outdated, their feathered hats a quiver
with gossip and gospel, their sturdy arms
full of pies, fried chicken, and green gelatin
thick with canned pear halves, walnuts,
and Jesus. Out there where the black-faced
statues of deferential jockeys lined white-rock
lanes around the park. Expectantly, they bowed
beneath the elms every fifty feet, hands held out
as if to hold the reins of some rich man's horse,
or gather a penny tip, then diffidently dip
their heads to murmur "Yassir." Some statues
stood guard at the dark pond where small,
bright fish and larger black fish struggled
for breath together among the choking
water lilies. They attended the white-painted
bandstand set among imposing centenary elms.
They were just a part of the park, less interesting
than the forlorn bear cage where we pale children
played tag and peered down through iron bars
at the dim dungeon below, where decades before
some sad animal had been chained. Black children—
some I knew from school—squealed and ran
in and out of the turbid water along a strip
of rocky, gritty beach, glimpsed only from a rowboat
rented from our side, on the far shore of the lake.

II.

Elm Town was ignorant of what was and what was
to come: the first diseased tree discovered
on a boulevard near the center of town, where old elms
gathered around the even older college, an aging family
of still virile gentlemen whose wizened faces
seemed to peer into the future and see what lay
there—inevitable, yet unfathomable. Polio,
too, threatened—a thing too small to see, yet larger
than life itself when viewed through a mirror
attached to an iron lung. So my father took us
three Sabin Sundays to stand in long lines
in the gymnasium, black and white waiting together
for the cure soaked into sugar cubes like the squares
my father brought me from hotels in Chicago
or Peoria, wrapped neatly in fine paper, tucked
into his leather valise. We swallowed the bitter-
sweet remedy, despised the taint of medicine,
while outside in the Lombard yard, the giant elm
(second largest in the country)—breathed
in our useless breaths, returning the life-
giving oxygen—stood tall, still vibrant
at ninety. Soon, Old Ben would fall
to the epidemic, the DDT-cure ineffective
and dangerous. Unmindful, we walked out
into a town of ten thousand elm trees
spreading their strong summer canopies of green
over the streets, their shadows dappling
the oblivious brick that, too, would soon be gone,
obliterated beneath a smothering caul of asphalt.

Christina Lovin

Shells

My father once took us to a cottage by the Mississippi—
my mother, my youngest brother, two or more
of an older brother's children—a boy and a girl,
if not more of each—their parents fighting again,
or divorced by then: another sister-in-law
to disappear, the promise of a new one on the air.
The weather was cool—the river below lethargic,
clinging with frozen fingertips to the impassive shore
while we shivered at night in the corners of the cabin,
stringing shells callously emptied of snails on leather laces
to wear like natives under striped blankets we hung
over clothesline—a thin cord that split the rafters' spaces.

By day, sunlight spread thin as ice on the path to the shore.
We walked to stay warm toward Oquawka, past a crossroads
I remember well—pines gossiped coldly, tall on all sides,
crowding the rutted lanes where two roads crossed, littered
with ruined shells from the button factory. Shells that filled
low places in the road: opalescent pink, creamy and smooth
as flesh. Muscle and meat of clams once clung there,
secluded in their rough armor like young girls' hearts
can be. How they grow up. Punched with holes—
any usefulness in the parts taken away, blank-faced
until carved and shot through, pierced and sewn to hearts
of strangers—the cast-off shells lay broken underfoot.

Parul Kapur Hinzen

In the Green Rain

I came here to see ghosts, but not the ones I found. I came to see the ghosts of Hindu gods in Khmer sculptures and the ways those gods have influenced the people. I didn't imagine the rebel ghosts of violence still holding people hostage. Death is no ghost in Cambodia, in this village, though some call it a spirit who won't leave. On a whitewashed wall surrounding the home of the area's oldest resident someone has drawn a moon face with a mouth flowing out of shape and long eyes weeping.

In the mornings, children run in the lane, gazing at the graffiti, then race off to hide under their thatched houses raised on stilts, lying down in the crawl spaces with the cows. Sometimes they chase after UN helicopters clattering across the sky. I pass the old lady's house on my way to the polling station. Beside the grieving image on the wall are drawings of the serene faces of divinities, their eyes closed to the world. I walk down the asphalt road wrapped in scarves, passing green pools mirroring green trees. Dark stumps of stone in the distance might once have been pagodas.

French teachers would make suitable polling officers in this ruined old colony of Indochina, the international organization decided, so I applied for a contract. I have an ambition, I've discovered, to accumulate textiles, to build an empire of hand-loomed cloth. I'm a high school teacher from Virginia, though that doesn't mean what it suggests. I was born in India and my marriage, now dead, began with two of us tied to each other by a pink sash as we circled the wedding fire.

Across the veranda of the school that serves as our polling station, my staff has strung buntings of paper flags, celebrating the country's first election. I monitor the silent faces queued up to cast ballots. It will take all week. My interpreter, Chhaya, elegant in her long, straight skirts, offers me papaya and cold drinks in the heat, but she's afraid to pass on any bad news I should know about. I sit in the veranda in my flak jacket, listening for mortar fire. If there's fighting, I will have to shut the school.

I am in charge. I am the boss of these shy ghosts. Many in their parents' generation were killed, sometimes with pickaxes to save on bullets. The gaunt young Khmer men on staff inspect the voters' photo IDs and let me manage the CPP men. Party agents menace the crowds, demanding to see voter cards, snatch them away. They hang around in their party T-shirts to let people know that Viet Nam, thirty kilometers to the south, is watching them. I knot a scarf around my head like a guerilla and stare the CPP men in the eye. They're too cunning and greedy to slide away like shadows. Chhaya, with her thick, sensuous mouth translates my snarling French into Khmer: "Get out of here, guys! Get lost! Free and fair elections. You understand?"

Staff officers pass on rumors they have heard. The CPP has attacked a village some distance down the asphalt road. People living along the river heard gunfire at night and saw flames rising from the Muslim town on the other side. Perhaps it's only their imaginations or their memories.

In the evenings, Chhaya accompanies me to the market so I can buy armloads of fabric, coarse red and green-checked Khmer scarves, cottons in bright prints. We're like twins, moving together, speaking in tandem, except she giggles over everything, especially my attempts at bargaining, and I'm numbed by how much pain she accepts.

One morning she takes me to the riverbank behind the market. She's heard of a vendor who sells a brilliant purple cloth from his canoe. Through the heavy mist I think I see a green rain blowing in the distance. Chhaya says it's only the pigment of the trees and grasses swirling in the atmosphere like ashes. She says you can capture ghosts in cloth. There are women in the village who believe their babies still live in the scarves they used to sling them in. "My father used to swim across the river in Kampong Trabek," she tells me. It's the district town where they'd lived. Quickly she silences herself, turning her veil of black hair to me, as if she's said too much already and turned to stone.

Mark McKain

Eating Albatross

> *Shot* Diomedea exulans, *wandering albatross;*
> *this we reckon a great acquisition to our bird collection.*
> —Sir Joseph Banks, February 1769

Unwell these three or four days,
treating myself with lemon juice and Brandy,
liquor shocking the nose, gums puffed and discolored,
confined to this closet that ached with the heave of the sea.

Mildew, fevered sweat. The medicine
working and now an emptiness, a space to taste
what I had shot before stomach wretched.
The bird's aroma strong, welcoming,
a sprig of seaweed decorates the breast.
I pray—

> *Will we never understand how*
> *pelagic birds are designed*
> *to live out in the ocean,*

> *how they enjoy the gale-force*
> *caressing angular wings? Nowhere to perch,*

resting
on wave's
inner thigh
as if curves
and chaos
were solid earth,
they search for krill
that love frigid water, extra oxygen,
perverse daylight—blood of the Southern Ocean.

*

From my skiff
the great bird tacks and glides,
long feathered bones tangential to ocean's curve—
am I already witnessing
the transit of Venus across the low sun?

Flint sparks, the muzzle reports,
and now its bedraggled wings
touch the deck. We weigh and measure,
fix its celestial mechanics, improve
our earthly navigation with its exquisite equation.

Now I must dine—so good that
everybody commended and eat heartily of them.
To Tahiti we must hurry;
the shadow of Venus will not wait
for another wandering albatross.

Mark McKain

Deception Island

after Hayashi Fumiko

Bone of whalebone,
kelp and sea ice stranded by the tide.
Leaping from the gray waves (hats, purses, hand warmers,
livers and hearts a delicacy) chinstrap penguins dance.
Weddell seal thrashes a fish head.
                     The rusty digesters,
that refined them for oil, list and sink; the dinghy drowns
in volcanic sand, the workers' hut exploded by a slurry of pumice.
                   A picket fence along the beach
still holds ghosts of meat and skin, vertebrae growing
through black sand, *as waves play along an invisible spine*;
stools to sit, drums to beat, steps to the bleached skull,
sailing toward the bay, once crowded with carcasses,
waters red; now inside an arc of ribs—
                  immense emptiness of a single blue.

Mark McKain

To His Sister

                    Sitting in the ship's library,
just embarked from Tierra del Fuego,
passing through the Beagle Channel, wondering
if Fuego's naked face, your poor kitty, is healing,
remembering my last visit, "moments when
I see myself naked under the gaze of the cat,"
and now riding the Southern Ocean's
three meter swells,

                    thinking on the Fuegians—
how they fished in rough boats, water running
off greased skin, but after adopting Western dress,
caught their death from sea-soaked clothes,
and even Charles, studying the zoophytes in the shallows,
could not stop from classifying them as less evolved,
a lower intelligence for lack of linen, excess skin—

                    but this disturbs less than
on first looking into Magellan's Narrative Account
where some "high persons" demand,
even beg for the intestines of a captured,
now dead, native to salve their wounds,
this journal sitting uneasily on my gut, as the ship falls
through gray seas toward the zero degree
convergence (here Darwin and the Beagle
turned north to the Galapagos, and the survival of …),

                    the sooty albatross,
tailing us since the channel, streaks past amidships
then turns again to hunt for bits of zooplankton,
stirred up by the propellers' turbulence,

                    and I imagine, dear sister,
you here, camera ready, quick to capture the slender,
magnificent wingspan (which you so love)
and we, under their dark gaze, standing, like Fuego
or the Fuegians, vulnerable, naked, cold, happy
inside with Brandy, to you scribbling.

<u>Mark McKain</u>

To His Father†

Wail from the colony like pumps, engines, valves clacking in refineries
where you worked. Find music in the gentoo's machine-like bray.

Humpback's gasp as it spouts. Our guide tells how she unwound fishing line
from a tangled pectoral fin. The times your reel would backlash.
Bird's nest, you said. Then it waved good-bye.

Devoted to daily experiences in small notebooks. A square port window onto
albatross flight, the gray sea swells to three meters, birds resting on the liquid slope.
Equations made me cry as you helped solve for x and y.

Crepuscule of blue touched with gold. Pleasant dinner chatter. Scribbling notes,
spun by an internal centrifuge to the perimeter. *I wish I had the opportunity to
devote myself entirely to collecting plants.*

Pianissimo of summer snow. *The utter desolation of 70 degrees south
could never have been expected.*

Human structures intruding and collapsing. Terns perched on the rim of a wrecked
freighter. Taking photos, amassing hundreds of images. Remember the first SLR
you carried in a green knapsack?

This is my main reason for devoting my time to the Crustaceae. Penguins surface
beside the kayak. Do they remember the slaughter? Childhood crayfish, tail and carapace
part of my reason. Your arm bringing up the net filled with waving pinchers.

Albatross gliding in ship's wake aged into a cloud. Tell them I am writing
about animals and family although not traveling with you, sister, wife or anyone
I know. *I hope the drawings I sent home will show I do not neglect you.*

The sheathbill, our guide says, is his favorite bird: stands on one foot,
does not have webbed feet, steals coins from the gift shop. Whistling a tune,
I had performed an Orpheus's part—twenty of these birds gathered around me.

Echoing crack (heard in the gut) of an iceberg calving. Crying, braying,
breaking the music of this sphere. *Until your last letter, I feared I was physically
incapacitated for the high trust reposed in me.* Midnight growlers scrape the keel.

In the ship's library I read how early explorers suffered, the suffering inflicted,
like skua or sheathbill, preying and collecting. Nunataks, stark black peaks,
inhabited by glaciers, watch our passage through the fjord.

Snow petrel, streaking past on Christmas Day. You gave up the guitar
to become an engineer to make a different music. *I do not care that my collections
should be mentioned in the public journals, as all I care for is to please you.*

Heart opens, melting, lost and roaming. *This splendid Burning Mountain
issues continually vast clouds of smoke.* My voice between your guitar and bird/whale
song, the fracture of the glacier, plunging into the sea.

† Italicized lines from the letters of Joseph D. Hooker.

Travis Mossotti

Red Wolf Capture

When we stepped inside the wolves' broad enclosure
I slid my forearm through the baffleboard's
leather straps, held it like a flimsy shield
against the dull winter chill, the wolves
looking down at us, beyond us and the fence
behind us for any means of possible escape.

　　　　But this was a routine capture, no room for escape,
　　　　and the unflappable walls of the chain-link enclosure
　　　　conspired with barbed wire on the lip of the fence
　　　　to make our work so easy: a few wooden boards,
　　　　a catchpole, a piece of cloth to cover the wolf's
　　　　eyes once we'd separated him from parents, his shield.

Twelve of us made a line, a literal human shield
ascending a snow-covered hill, the landscape
of those Missouri hills written into the wolves'
DNA, each breath rising from the enclosure
as if they'd never been extirpated from the broad
chest of the Midwest, as if there were no fences.

　　　　And when the young male broke away down the fence
　　　　line, I let him run past me, then turned to shield
　　　　his retreat. Our tactics were simple: use the board
　　　　to corner him; slip the catchpole around the nape
　　　　of his neck; mind the surroundings and make sure
　　　　his mother and father stayed at a safe distance. Wolves

mind you, are instinctually wary of humans, but wolves
are also savvy predators, fence or no fence,
that can exert a bite pressure of 1500psi, and the enclosure's
design made it tricky to see them at all times, tricky to shield

encroachment. I even began to consider avenues of escape
while the team drew blood, wrote on a clipboard,

> the young animal given over to the bored
> complacency of despair. Eventually that wolf
> I helped to capture was released, escaped
> Missouri for the Alligator River National Wildlife Refuge,
> no fences framing the limits to his world, no fences shielding
> him from hunters, ranchers or highway traffic. That enclosure

designed to shield wolves from the politics
of extinction. That enclosure and the broad lengths
of chain-link fence. Those hills, that winter landscape.

Travis Mossotti

Fossil Rim Wildlife Center
—Glen Rose, Texas

For over fifty years the mock African savannah
seeped in
to the dry hills of Fossil Rim,
and while I ran a few miles in the morning,

working up a sweat,
kudu, black buck, wildebeest,
giraffe and zebra
watched me with one eye,

the sun watching us all
as though we presented
an odd juxtaposition,
nothing it hadn't seen before.

If this had been Africa
I would have been on safari,
but this was America,
or Texas at least,

so this was just another business day
where mail arrived
on time at an office
to be sorted,

the letter I had sent Regina
before leaving Illinois
arriving after I had
like a herd of gazelle

chasing a rain cloud
long gone,

already flooding
another stretch of desert.

Over one hundred degrees
at barely nine o'clock.
It might have actually been Africa:
Northern Kenya, Tanzania,

the Namibian desert,
the cradle   of civilization
Regina dreamed
of returning to each night,

each morning waking up somewhere else:
    another cheetah enclosure,
        another set of behaviors to chart,
            another possible conclusion

as to why mating
proved so difficult
in captivity: the stress,
the courtship gone.

As I ran, I kept thinking
about the howler monkey
we saw the day prior,
the belly of mesh wire

that slowly digested him,
started with the eyes,
making them hollow,
the rest of him left

to wither on display
for the education
and amusement
of another school bus

weighed down
with eager minds
eager for the thing
in the cage with a sign on it:

a Latin name,
a native habitat
it would never see
in this lifetime or the next.

After only two miles the heat had clearly gotten to me, and when I got back, Regina said to put on swim trunks, said that we were going for a swim at Dinosaur Valley State Park. The park was just a mile down the road, and there was a slow bend in the river that made a good swimming hole—footprints of the extinct imprinted in bedrock. At the entrance to the park sat a Creation Evidence Museum begging, by way of billboard, for an opportunity to dispel the rumors of old bones and Darwinian logic, for free, five days a week:

                              six thousand years of existence
                                    packed into a darkened room:
                              Adam and Eve,   a matching
                                    set of fig leaves, her forearm

                                          shading her nipples
                                              and the shame
                                          of feeding her young
                                              like an animal.

When we got to the spot,
we had to hike barefoot
down a slim dirt path
to the rocks and water below.

Regina took off her shirt and said
occasionally the cheetahs
attacked each other
instead of mating,

that it was a waste of genetics
and money to ship
an incompatible mate
three thousand miles.

Just then I put my foot inside
a *Tyrannosaurus rex* footprint,
slid my heel into his
and felt it go the length of my spine:

a creeper winding up
a desiccated oak tree
in search of sunlight
during the fallout

of that first nuclear winter
after a comet
punctuated the Gulf of Mexico,
millions of unspeakable years

before I watched
a chubby Latino kid
do a cannonball
into the river,

backstroke
to the shore, the sun
glistening the round
of his upturned belly.

Part of me wished
there actually was
a divine garden
so pure

it only breathed in light
filtered by the lungs of God—
the sterility

of eternity

somehow beautiful enough
to give up a lifetime
of afternoons
at the swimming hole.

But another part of me
couldn't stop staring
at the brilliant white
of Regina's breasts covered

by a slim red top—
an almost saintly gesture.
I dove headlong
out of the footprint

into the cool of the river,
felt its weak current
under my feet as I floated in twilight,
waiting for her to dive in,

waiting for that ancient water
to fill in around us.

Elizabeth Deanna Morris

In-Grown

As a way to decompose bodies, a way to bring us back
to loam, a scientist shrouds a woman's body with mycelium,
a blanket like white cotton candy/fiber glass, and sprinkles
spores across. The humidity floats as if it could
be rain, were we not in a lab: a box of Plexiglas: bright
lights: filtered unending sun. Spores swell to mushrooms
along the plane of her stomach like a skyline pushes away
from its horizon, and then their caps pull open
like this now-dead woman once lifted her skirt above the dirt
on the forest floor.

                                        *

*In the dream that night, I see the mushrooms poking
out from underneath the collar of his shirt. I look
more closely, straining to see through the white cotton.
The mushrooms are growing all over his stomach
and chest. They grow out and up, recreating the upward
move from gravity. I think, "Oh God, oh God, they're in
him now." I think, "He can't go back." We cannot remove
them without pulling away layers of skin,
fat. He will decompose while still alive.*

Elizabeth Deanna Morris

In-Grown

In dividing the fruit: his teeth like small stone hatchets
left out, mossy with plaque: he split the firm
pink guava into bites. The pebbly seeds rolling
across his tongue, except one which found a nestling-
cranny in the back tooth: one so chiseled inward
that the guava seed hooked into place: and warm
and wet, germinated, sinking roots against the root
of tooth, poking a single leaf out, reaching
toward mouth to where it might find some light.

*

*In the dream that night, the roots of the guava tree
have already sunk into my throat, like a cavern unearthed,
dripping. Other things are trying to settle into place,
strings of clear jelly encasing black, toad's eggs keep appearing
when I sleep, lining the space between my gum and lip. I pull them out
like pearls. With the long nail on my index finger,
I scoop the lady bugs that crowd the
arch in my ear. I know my fingers
will soon no longer be dexterous enough, quick enough.*

Elizabeth Deanna Morris

In-Grown

After six years, immobile, the woman's skin grafted
to the couch where she sat. Beneath her: feces, maggots,
rot, sores that coned in like strip mines. A swamp
of human and couch. Four-hundred and eighty pounds
of living flesh on brown chenille fabric: putrefying.
The paramedics took a scalpel to the cushion, but her body
consumed too much, intertwined like clasped fingers. A wall
was removed, the couch:woman carried through.
Forty-years-old, she died at the hospital, unable
to reject her non-human parts.

*

In my sleep that night, I did not dream,
did not dream of babies growing and dying,
of plants ingesting my body. Instead, when I
woke in the darkness, my right arm was numb underneath my ribs.
Kenny, asleep beside me, did not stir.
My blood vibrated beneath my ribs. When I squinted
through the grayness at the numbness, it was a conscious
act to remember that it was mine. I rubbed my good hand along
the numb arm, as if this would hurry back
the blood.

Damyanti Ghosh

Fire Extinguished

Take the day off, they said, her sisters, You're no good at the pole tonight, and Shelly left. She took off the feathered costume at a go, instead of bit by teasing bit to reveal her brown skin like she did each evening. This time nobody watched her. Not when she took off her painted face, nor the eyelashes that batted and winked, bringing wolf whistles, drunken cheers and dollar bills.

But at her apartment she found no peace because that wasn't where she wanted to be, but thousands of miles away, further than any one could walk or fly in time. No use for that bottle of wine now, the one she'd saved up and bought to tell her father she loved him, she'd done him proud at the Big Apple even though he couldn't afford her college fees. To celebrate their meeting they would drink themselves silly on a bottle of Barolo he longed to buy but couldn't afford, and try not to miss her mother.

Now that she won't need to pretend, might as well wear this sedate black office dress she'd bought to go pick him up from the airport, and perhaps stretch her restless legs in the park in front of her building block. He told her not to walk out late at night, it wasn't safe. But what could they threaten her with? She had lost much, starting with her name, hardly anything left to lose.

She grabbed the bottle of wine and walked out on staid pump shoes. So much easier than stilettoes. She kicked them off to walk on the grass, and when the wine wouldn't let her walk, she sat down, cross-legged, Indian style, the way her father did at prayers, and all her people.

Right now, they must be taking him to the flames. It is 3 pm in India. The family would wear white, and whisper to each other about Sheela in America who couldn't make it to the funeral.

His brothers would call their wives from the burning ghaat once he'd returned to the dust from where he came, and the fire had been extinguished. The womenfolk would wash the house, and take their ritual bath. His daughter would be the only one sitting halfway across the world getting drunk, bone dry other than her eyes.

Eyelids squeezed shut, she didn't see the first splash coming. But then she spread her arms out at the sprinklers, letting them bathe her. From time to time she took a swig of his favorite wine, water flowing over her face in cold rivulets.

Lenore Weiss

Cancer Survivor in the City

The city
etched her face
into a pie chart

wedges of a nose,
mouth,
eyes shadowed,

each an escapee
from the big
picture,

a radioactive half-life
not counting
piano bars hidden

beneath subways,
black keys
minoring in months

until some metronome
in Central Park
at a water fountain

leaned her mouth
close in
for a single sip

as her parents stood
on either side
raised left and right

hand and lifted
her feet off
the ground.

Lenore Weiss

Eastern Tiger Swallowtail

> *Coincidences of pattern is one of the wonders of nature.*
> —Vladimir Nabokov

The same evening he plugged himself
into an amplifier and lit up
with the neon of his young manhood,
there all the time in the background,

as she searched for a place to rest
with the pressure of metamorphosis
knocking her out cold on the concrete patio
making it difficult in the next few weeks
to wash her hair or sit up straight in bed

reading how Nabokov
had snuffed out the life of silver-studded
butterflies and smelled the vanilla and musk
perfume of their wings on his fingertips.

She got better. He continued to play,
a bass guitar streamed from his own fingertips
smelling of her hair even as he dug a hole
in the backyard where a spider plant revolved
around its own hook.

She went to sleep and bathed herself,
an infant child in the dim light of a dream,
knew it had to be her by the startled look.

The next morning an Eastern Tiger Swallowtail
outside the garage with black wings and a blue band
sampled Hosta for hours, and wouldn't go away.

Mary Senger

The Day the Blackbirds Fell

The blackbirds fell today.

It happened in the dead of night; nobody saw a thing. We all woke and found what had happened; small black bodies scattered across the concrete and asphalt.

The newscasters told us it was bad weather, clouds confused them, lighting startled or electrocuted them, hail knocked them out of the sky, they froze mid-air, their bad eyesight coupled with these explanations may have caused them to fly straight at the earth.

The conspiracy theorists told us the government has poisoned them. They said nuclear testing had killed them with radiation. They claimed it was the beginning of an alien invasion. They said witches were brewing up a storm.

They told us that the end was coming.

The historians reminded us about the flamingos, the blue jays and the common pigeons that had died en masse in the past. The tense air that had been building up in everyone's lungs finally escaped and people returned to cubicles, business reports, and five o'clock traffic. There was nothing to worry about. It was a strange, natural phenomenon, that was all. Jokes had already circulated and died like blood cells.

Nobody noticed when all the fish in Lake Michigan died, or when the birthrate dropped 20%. The tsunami in Hawaii was a natural occurrence, perfectly explainable, despite its span. Everyone had been expecting earthquakes in California. People blamed the spoiled foods in their refrigerators on the power outages. They blamed the power outages on the bad weather; tornadoes in January and hailstorms in April. And everyone complained that the gas prices kept rising.

In the meantime, no one remembered the prophesy that began, "When the blackbirds fall ..."

Frances Gapper

Cleaner

It was an end-of-tenancy cleaning job. She'd been sent by the agency. On arrival, she looked around her in dismay, then set to work. The whole place was filthy, littered with discarded packaging and crawling with pests. Shuddering, she averted her eyes while following vermin control procedures. The agency had been remiss—this should have been done ages ago. However, at last all the bugs were dead. She vacuumed up the forests, siphoned the oceans, bagged what remained and put it all into deep storage.

Matt Rotman

Dreams of Crooked Cigarettes

Perhaps there was a point if not for all the pointlessness. An S-curve, the car sloped around, upward, penetrating the darkness like ascending the vertical section of a quarter slinky. The headlights made headway, the branches of trees broke vision, and when they had to stop, a peculiar mission, indeed, setting them in some direction:

> *How weird words were*
> *like Wordsworth in pursuit,*
> *perched, unwavering, unlocked;*
> > *a spoodle spaniel poodle,*
> > *the Star-spangled Banner,*
> *upkeep, uncouth banter—In the isles,*
> *sheepish and seasick, synchronicity bears*
> > *that of gold, glad to be*
> > *oversold and rotting—or what it appears*
> *or was already.*

More sense it would have made if there were snow, but just footsteps on pavement, ghosts on the road, except there were no ghosts, only road. In the dark, it sounded like fleeting, with the beer, it felt like courage, though they crept in like war. For it wasn't for them, you see, neither was it far, the floods taking away the tar like uncertain fathers in curtained dens. An homage to pornography, similar to the heavens fashioning the sky:

> *It was the Mark of Cain,*
> *a paternal prank in any sense,*
> *a wish, macabre, to say the least,*
> > *though God listened as he*
> > *sent the rain, whistled as he*
> *made the list, martyrs without feet*
> *drowned in old age.*

Profanity used religiously, he thought, can make one helluva powered wheeled plane. Instead, he said, you can tell it rained, though his friend rebutted as if having to, I can see his car. Flashlights swung, almost catching the waters receding, mud retching stunk, and fireflies flew meaninglessly, and it hung on the ground motionlessly. Newborn is to reborn, he thought, and water turns dirt into mud. He remembered a hymn his mother used to sing to him:

but she said at night they break
and turn to fog—
on the ground, they are images
of my breath,
and in the light, things that grow
just to die.
A sea breaks down in territories
to kick and scream—
Things that swim through me don't enter
into the air. But I do.

In retching mud, it's a weird remembrance, an anniversary perhaps, to peel human off the embankment. But it's just ghosts and the road, but no road and only ghosts. And to go forward is to move fluidly and move worrying is just moving. He said, in his last hand, he folded with ace king diamond connectors. Up to his neck in mud, his friend cornered, yeah, because he loved poker. Pointing to nothing, he said, shine your light over there:

Oh, Hail Mary, full of space,
the morgue has a lease
on our fathers who art within
hallow be thy dilapidation,
and the life that it leads.

To follow a cross to the T, across the creek, a bumper sat aimless and grinning, tracks of a natural borne path glistened, though man made stuck to the air like marmalade. Sickened, our hero tries to wash the feeling off in the water which receded yesterday:

I dreamt of crooked cigarettes
getting their fix off fears,
determined to deflect the shame.

Judith Skillman

My Pocket Gopher

It wasn't so bad before he began digging
his way in. We lived for years like the married,
avoided sensitive areas, knew
the taboos. His cheek pouches held memos
I wrote but couldn't send to the others.
Better than a shredder, more secure. He
only left my shirt late at night to work
the tunnels honeycombed under the house,
a system of branched opening sealed
tight with earthen plugs. At dawn he returned
to my shirt. His stripes matched the pinstripe
costume I selected from a closet
open year round, full of the same shirt
pronouncing its brand name on a tag sewn
right next to the bulge his compact body
made. I didn't mind the company though
we both preferred to be alone, away
from our widespread families—the fresh soil
in mounds to advertise what would've been better
left unknown. Flower beds, lawns, gardens—all
fair game to the habits of damage. I
grew to love the familiar ritual
of his return, worried he'd be cropped
by legalities. In order to keep
the gopher safe I thought we were a pair.
I managed my small orchard obsession-
style, never invaded members of my
own family with bait though God knows
they deserved it. Carrots, apples, lettuce—
none of these kept my gopher from eroding
the world I could see. It was the inner
place, those wires driven like probes in between
the confidence I projected like

poison, sooner and better than sister
or brother: it was the inside the gopher
was after. As tenant of my body
how could I locate the drop in moistness?

How to eradicate experiences
honed by dowels and diameters, set
like the two-pronged pincher or Macabee
trap, the choker-style box that would inflict its
lethal click to keep my pocket gopher
from ever getting in, ever penetrating
even one iota of volcanic
activity just beneath the skin, those
outwardly soft surfaces infected
by motherhood and lips.

Judith Skillman

Paganini's Pinky

Like a rodent's tail it trails the carriage: flesh-toned,
long enough to anchor the right hand in its death cast.

Engorged with pebbles, like the frog of a horse—sensitive,
callous-shod, poised to fable four octaves and double back for pizzicato.

Then again it's only a quirk of nature, a by-product, symptom
of Marfan's disease, Syphilis, Ehlers-Danlos syndrome, or speculation.

If mute, he'll enter the concert hall as pale as he is tall
to play the part of a witch's child, his back bowed by scoliosis.

Suppose the pinky dangles inside his skinny black braid,
anchors the fingerboard, an ebony bone gone gangrenous.

The four black horses run on stones beneath the moon.
A long sinuous road carries the maestro who bangs around

inside his cage as all of him becomes loose, lax,
pliant enough to execute whatever romance requires.

Amanda Larson

Only Embers

Sand constantly shifted. It pushed up between Kakuve's toes as she walked across the village, carrying a gourd filled with water. The breeze had yet to warm with the sun only starting to peer over the great dunes on the horizon.

Those dunes had been crafted by wind and time, both of which had once seemed an ally. Together, they brought the rains that sustained her people and quenched the Namibian desert's thirst.

Kakuve poured some of that precious water into the cooking pot. It was a cast iron pot, purchased from a distant market. It was one of many things that didn't belong. As she crouched down beside it, her knees creaked. Time wasn't always a friend.

One of her daughters emerged from the hut with a fresh application of red otjize paste decorating her skin from head to toe. The shells and copper of Matutjavi's necklace and bracelets clanked as she bounced her son on her hip.

On the surface, the world Kakuve's grandson had been born into looked unchanged from the one of her birth. They lived as they always had, carrying the embers of the ancestral fire as they followed the cattle wherever the wind took them. The barren desert still stretched from horizon to horizon, but it wasn't barrier enough.

Matutjavi set down her son before crouching to milk a cow. While Kakuve stirred the porridge, she watched the boy crawl through the sand. He plopped down beside a plastic bottle that had been left by the last group of tourists who had found them. He giggled as he beat the crushed bottle against the hut's wall.

For some, the wind had stopped blowing. Fewer and fewer traveled the lands of their ancestors. Nomadic villages became stagnant and dependent on outsiders. Their children were taught in towns by new elders who didn't speak to the ancestors.

Motors rumbled in the distance, a harsh sound cutting through the pristine silence of the morning. Their village had chosen solitude, but still the world sought them out.

Several cars came into view over the rise. The children dropped firewood they'd been carrying or left the goats they'd been watching to peer through the village's wall at the approaching visitors.

When she'd been a child, her people had been strong. Wars and droughts had come and gone and still the Himba remained. She'd never questioned that their ancestral fire would always burn.

Now she knew there would be no more generations to carry on the fire. Her grandson would be the last. Like the sand, the winds constantly shifted. Time continued on. She couldn't stop the world that came, but she could live as she always had until the fire went out.

Sarah Fawn Montgomery

Losing Ground

Just north of Iiulissat, on Greenland's fjordy coast,
a glacier frees itself from the surface, leaves
the country and slides into the sea like a glossy seal
moving towards a bright point on the water, never resurfacing.

News stations report this the latest sign of self-made apocalypse:
the land we stand on disappearing.

Some warn of the warming, liken it to the island of Elugelab
displaced by atomic blast, or mining strips of land like peeled sunburn.
But this has happened before—coiled fossil shells litter deserts,
mountains shift their heights. Besides, the dodo was clumsy.

Redraw the maps, reimagine the borders.
The resting ground is gone, the ocean slightly higher for the trade.

Sarah Fawn Montgomery

A Surviving Letter from the *Hindenburg*

The letter rode upon the airship
like a barnacle on the back of a whale,
or a shoal of prey caught in strands of baleen.

The airship moved as if the sky were water,
pushing through wind and cloud cover,
a blowhole burst of gas and steam disrupting silence.

Suddenly, as though a harpoon struck,
the beast blazed, a blue flume of flame at its fin.
No lash of tail, no surge of water.

In but a minute, the body engulfed—
a mushroom swell of blooming smoke—
and the entrails of the whale-ship fell from the sky.

The letter fluttered, flamed from the blue,
past spectators, eyes craned to the gentle ruined creature.

Jennifer Clark

Longing for the Dynamite Days

It was a time when one had the luxury of nursing
a fondness for TNT, could

give in to one's penchant for throwing
pies in the face
or, on days when a little more felt in order, build
a Burmese tiger trap

ordered from ACME,
a good old American Company
that Made Everything.

Ah, to know your nemesis
like Tweetie knew Putty Cat,
Jerry knew Tom and that never-veering-from-the-road
Road Runner knew Wile E. Coyote.

You could always count on them being up to
something looney somewhere.

It was a time when gravity
was the greatest thing to fear
a plank of wood wedged under a boulder
teetering high on the cliff above one's head.

Characters folded flat, slim as dollar bills
tucked into the warmth of your wallet,
crumpled like muslin, turning up
with nary a crease in the next exchange.

The worst to be suffered was humiliation
in this simpler time of cactus and road
dog houses, aprons and chicken coops.

Everyone never quite succeeding
but never giving up.

As re-runs play over and over
mailboxes, you worry, are becoming a thing of the past.

Susan Sailer

Bouquet of Language: Losing Petals[†]

Of 7,358 living languages, 90% will be extinct
by 2050. Every 14 days one goes silent.

Yesterday the last fluent speaker of Pazeh, today
no one on Taiwan speaks it. Her language students
meet, can't pronounce the words without her tongue
to guide them through the sounds.

Eighty-five, he sits in a worn easy chair. Outside,
prairie wind rustles elm leaves, raises dust on West
Tulsa streets. Photos line his living room wall—
warrior in headdress on a galloping pony, dancing
women in beaded deerskin dresses. Above his head
a dreamcatcher hung with eagle feather, red beads,
badger's foot. The last native speaker of Euchee,
he knows that when he dies his language dies.

                                    *

When a language goes extinct, who mourns?
Is language loss like species loss? Dwarf
elephant, giant beaver, pallid beach mouse,
La Brea stork, Catahoula salamander, golden
toad, saber-toothed salmon. Livonian, Aka-Bo,
Nooksack, Manx, Tasmanian, Kemi Sami, Old Nubian.

In Brazil, the Pirahãs language has eight consonants,
three vowels, but its 300 living speakers don't use
these sounds, instead they hum, whistle, sing their
conversations using syllable lengths, stresses, tones.
Did Aka-Bo have words for 3? 100? Or did few
and *many* do the job? Did Old Nubian have words
for 40 shades of brown? Could I have said *I love you*

so sweetly as to be your sugar always?

Isabel Chavela Torres to the Field Linguist:
The world outside El Desemboque and Punta
Chueca calls us Seri but we call ourselves
Comcaac. Our home has always been what lies
between the desert and the sea. We fish, hunt,
gather. Men carve sea turtles from ironwood
growing in the desert. We string shell necklaces,
weave baskets so tight no water leaks. What
there is—cactus fruit, eelgrass—we share. No one
owns much but what there is we bury with us.

Our language is Cmiique Iitom. We never wrote
before you came, we had no need. Everyone has
a flower inside, and inside the flower is a word.
I will help you find our words. On rare occasions
when we travel to strange villages we make a gesture
with our forearms raised to the sky, *ziix quih hasssax
haaptxo quih ano cocacaaixaj*, one who greets with joy
and peace and harmony. It shows we mean no harm.

On rare occasions when a stranger comes to us
we ask, *Miixoni quih zo hant ano tiij?* Where do
you come from, stranger? Where is your placenta
buried? Mine lies 40 steps outside my house,
dug into the ground, under sand and ash, topped
with two smooth rocks.

Our ceremonies come from *hant iiha cohacomxoj*.
I was given this knowledge, I pass it on. I taught
my grandson the deer dance, now he teaches it
to Comcaac children. He is *hepem coicooit*, one
who dances like the white-tailed deer. The daughter
of my younger grandson is *atcz*, but the daughter
of his older brother is *azaac*.

New power lines run through the desert to work

our pump at the village well. That brought strangers.
More will come. I fear our children will learn Spanish,
move away. Already some women go to hospitals to have
their babies. Who will we be if our language dies?

*

Aidyng Ozeeri Speaks:
I was training to be the Tofa's next shaman
but last month my father had a heart attack.
I know how to heal with plants for sickness,
I know drum beats for the cures and dances
but I hadn't learned to use seeds from feather
grass, leg bone from a pica, scent glands
from a musk deer, powder from a walrus tusk.
My father knew the chants. He talked to spirits,
found how to solve our problems. We have
become a tiny tribe, no more than 30.

When I was a boy, we were bigger but then
so many moved to Kyzyl to find jobs. Our Tuvan
cousins number in the many thousands—we too
ride reindeer, know how to sing in our throats
to make two sounds at once—but our language
is our own, it's hard to understand their speech.
The only good Tofa speakers are old. I speak
Russian better than Tofa. If my father lived,
I could have learned and taught the children.
Now I don't know what to do.

† Much of the information in this poem comes from Russ Rymer, "Vanishing
Voices," *National Geographic*, July 2012, 60-93.

John Gosslee

The Old Languages

a cassette tape and a printing press
talk on the telephone

the two-way mirror
is replaced with window glass

a shaman dons an owl headdress
and fans an eagle wing

the bar's cigarette smoke
calligraphy

John Gosslee

Portrait of an Inner Life

a mansion
inside a hovel

an elephant
trapped in a swallow

the claw at the end
of a roar

a frame
without a door

John Gosslee

Cold November

It's quiet on top of the rock at night.
The bees hibernate, the bare trees are winter's trophies.
I sneeze into the air and nothing comes out of my nose or mouth.
The moon is a hatchet blade in my eye.
It didn't look this glum in summer.
Inside my parka, it's as cold as my nose
and I feel the marble sized bees coiled for spring.
I fling a few into the air and they scramble towards the moonlight
until I can't see them anymore.

Ursula Villarreal-Moura

Menorca

At six a.m. I roused you and your brother from your twin beds. Our suitcases stuffed with Spanish souvenirs stood by the door. I would be your nanny for one day more then resume a place in the pink fog of your summer memories.

Already dressed in our airport clothes—a shortcut I'd decided would spare me the hassle of wrestling with our luggage—I shepherded us to the villa kitchen. Neither you nor your brother asked about your parents. The night before they'd requested to sleep in until four minutes before the taxi was due to arrive.

Knowing the overhead light bulb would be too stark, too cruel to our exhausted faces, I lit a votive candle on the counter. Like Catholics waiting for communion, you and your brother cupped your hands for breakfast.

Over our three-week stay we'd feasted on hamburgers and horchata, fish patties and French fries, but only reluctantly had I ponied up dessert. What would I feed you now at this pre-dawn hour? Your soft cheeks and ruffled eyebrows trusted me.

I handed you the only option that eliminated utensils and dishes: ice cream sandwiches. "Bon appétit," I said. "So cool" you and your brother muttered in unison as you raced each other to unwrap your treats. Figuring it would be half a day and another country until we ate again, I decided to have one, too.

Huddled in a triangle in the dim kitchen, we said nothing about the aching cold coating our teeth or about our collective disappointment in returning home. When you and your brother licked the last of the vanilla cream from the papery wrappers, in an attempt to delay the inevitable, I placed the ice cream box on the counter and told you both it was now or never.

Rebecca Clever

In Breaux Bridge, The Water Brings Us Together

Burdened with wisdom of the disappearing landscape, you pass the small,
solid cypress treasures you've salvaged, their ancient forms sanded smooth
as skin, give to our hands the texture of extinction.

Even as you speak, Monsieur Guirard, the coastal wetland sinks under
its own weight, your story immersed in depths that birthed you: the swamp,
its plot knit together in Spanish moss shadow.

The Atchafalaya Basin is flowing fields of water hyacinth, is empty shells
of trees hollow from grief, is cypress knees bowing in surrender, or reverence,
to the god of finite things.

Is your Louisiana, diminishing.

Rebecca Clever

Homage to the Hill,
Homage to August Wilson

Hill District folk feed on history, called it 'Sugartop'

when jazz ruled Crawford Square's clubs, Billy Strayhorn
Roger Humphries, George Benson drawing crowds
'til the City razed it in the name of *urban renewal*
pushing blacks—8,000 plus—to Swissvale, Homestead
Hazelwood, for what? An opera house-turned-
ice rink. Just down Crawford, then right up Webster

August was born. A Pulitzer on The Hill. Meager
beginnings for someone like him. Bricks
through windows taunted GO HOME NIGGER.
Tormented for uncommon skin, he penned
masterpieces from misery in steel town's libraries,
played out to rave reviews on stages. *Did he make*

his German baker papa-left-the-scene, Carolina
Deep-South-mama proud? White questions
to black answers they'll never understand, like
the thing about The Hill is people living there
are all looking to leave, maybe from the stress
of working in that *other* color world. It's about

what a place don't have and what folk do
to get around it. You get stepped on enough times
you get an attitude. Wilson was into the blues
and the causes for writing them. It's like he said:
it seems right to suffer a little, not as some
kind of martyr, so much as for empathy's sake.

Rebecca Clever

Facing Her

Decatur is boarded-up

shop windows, CLOSED
signs: SORRY, SHORT-STAFFED.
Rue de Vieux Carré testifying
trials of a broken city yet to see
300,000 displaced residents
return. Give me heat

Jackson Square flooded
in sunlight, a saxophonist
playing for change, though Katrina
owns it all, looter-routed
buildings, books & newspapers
people's conversation, their want

for reunion as homes are razed.
I thought I could not write Her
on postcards, planned to pen music
muffaletta, Mississippi mud. Even
in the ink She looms,
haughty apparition stalking me

through N'awlins' historic grid.
How to *laissez les bon temps rouller*
when block to block—St. Louis
to Toulouse, St. Peter to St. Ann
to Dumaine—are leftovers?
Barefoot junkie begging

in torn jeans, your tattered
sweater's sleeves fail

to hide arms fucked black & blue
by needles, Quarter strung
out on a Category 5 fix.
I call you Katrina

name the face of loss.

Rebecca Clever

When Henrietta Hoffman Stopped Speaking German

A stroke suppressed her mother tongue, handed down from immigrant parents
who outlawed spoken English in the house, so she dropped
the hard-edged words until the cold months
of her years.

She told us then how her Charlie ached for water: to swim against it, wrestle
with its muscle, cool off the body summers in the Monongahela.

Her lips knotted in recounting. *Verr hot dat day, ran down Vest Street's hill, 'cross da
Homestead train tracks to da river bank, dove in.*

Blood blossomed as clouds in the current when a boat's tow rope hooked
a nostril, tore the nose partly from his inflated face.

Did not vant it to be my child, but no one else's.

A milk truck rumbled in passing an alley over. She rocked in her crippled chair.

Ja, ja, once more, *mein sohn.* Rivers in her eyes.

J. Weintraub

Noah's Brontosauri

Yes, the sauropods were aboard, along for the ride,
and if they hadn't been such clumsy beasts—
always stumbling, tumbling, and falling over the side,
until no more than one remained of each—
they'd still be here to walk the earth.

They should've got their sea legs first,
or, at the very least, learned how to swim;
there were no life preservers quite their size
and no one ever saw them falling in,
and yet, on second thought, some have surmised:
perhaps not accidents, but suicides
by those who knew the world was no longer theirs.

But listen, and you'll hear rumors in the air
concerning plots that led to their demise,
cabals of small mammals, needing room to evolve,
and though such dark matters can be hard to resolve,
I doubt the dinosaurs volunteered a dive;
and though natural forces were surely still involved,
I believe they neither fell nor slipped,
but when the decks were pitch dark, and seas rolled high,
were surprised from below, were pushed, or tripped.

Lauren Camp

Pin-Wheeled *Descansos* in Taos

Where every man names
a street for himself, my friend and I
lurch a two-lane road toward
the blushing sky.
We roll by spectrums—
no nouns or verbs, just a mix
of colors cutting through
the shifting curves and brine of sun.
By dare or fear we take the earth fast,
passing the lingering scare
of chambered vanes
and their countless greetings.
On this long fall afternoon,
we drive gravel on streets scribbled
with corners where the road runs
to a banner of olive and sand,
to the middle of mountains,
the perfect piñon annex at 8,000 feet.
In the unanticipated gesture of bend
and swerve, we drive by bones
left in pieces. I can tolerate nothing
more small and haunting
than these symbols left to spin,
their eager petals placed in the point of grief,
and whirling witless in the wind.
Another sad story turning,
irrefutable, on the shoulder of dusty light.
Frothed clouds hang above
where people ghost, unfinished,
along the taut skin of rural ground.
The earth memorizes their forms and division,
their skids in the road.
With each turn of our wheel,

we move toward and away. How far
till we get there, till we break the surface?

Lauren Camp

Even Sound Can Disappear

A heavy man, squat with a shaved head—, he gave me
his single eye & sonorous sound
     puckered with pitch-dark thought.

Each day, he leaned
into an armchair & rolled his voice out
like a carpet

through a microphone to the long limbs of the city.
His feelings stepped gingerly from our speakers

& wrapped us while we made breakfast. His grief
formed the genial backdrop for our days, an improvised solo

of notes. Thoughts of wind
& traffic came tender, & twanged music

emerged from his tightened fists.
But his anger was inaudible—
     unless your ears were tuned.

I knew he mourned his deviations, knew
his voice shimmied & broke when he was alone. I knew he wept

without warning.
Those days, we talked radio all the time; I was a novice

at the mic of the master,
watching the quake & whistle of his breath,
more a shape than a sound:

learning how to exhale, inhale, tuck our listeners in.
He gained resonance by falling

into the steamy creek of his life. I couldn't hear the bottom,

                              & couldn't keep him from it.
Some nights he sat on my porch, sucking the mist
from a bottle of pilsner
with his fat pigmented lips,

the fogless night descending on us. We didn't touch.
And then he'd laugh

& the laughter would bend
          as the tantrum swooped down. As he rocked, I watched
him puddle in a single private color, sipping forward

until memory slipped out of him. The static
of what he couldn't tell me
left only his meeker skin behind.

Though he could vector his voice to fill his listeners,
he couldn't reach the one dream he hadn't heard

so he upended the color & shape of his name,
laid his vigorous tones by the window

& moved east
with a rubber-banded box of photographs.
He left his uncertain song in my mirror
          & seven volumes of contexts on my shelves.

                         *

     The city was so quiet.

     Sound stood still,
but we were steadier.
                    No more warnings.

I was alone with a microphone &
his sloped explanation of vibration:
       how we must allow a deep space for anger,
raise our head so the rectangle
                of uncertainty tumbles out
    & offer our wide open lung of longing.

              *

He called last week, his voice keeling
through the line: cloudy & sort of tilted. I didn't remember it this way;

charred, I would have said. Unremarkable.
It spiked. He said words anyone might have said.

He slid along backward, narrating years of factory work,
40 hours in a sanctuary of exhausted men, where he drives

a shopping cart through chain-red days & the nervy
razor-edge of oils & vapors & cups of day-old coffee. His small world

continues organizing in repetitive harmony;
seconds move in & out again.

Just like radio, they huddle up & make some noise.
Then disappear.

Lee Tyler Williams

Robert's Stonefly (*of a ghost taxonomy*)

As the stonefly haunts water, its circular assaults become more linear. Hovering outcroppings, its thorax mimics sallow moss and the blood of its wings swell to dirt crystal. It trails the narrowing course through banks of primeval ash trees when towns like Mackinaw and Goodfield and Colfax were flooded hamlets awaiting a depot or mineblast, clouding each path to the river. Unlike the flesh fly, it rises slower for the weight of its wings and lingers where the stream is ravenous, where children in white frocks are plunged and rafts abandoned, where window frames collapse with piled netting and the pans hanging beside the oven reek of fishgut.

Lee Tyler Williams

Dürer's Dream

The vision let him sleep again after the sweat had dried. The walls hollowed with the sound of rain and the wind unsettled the papers on the table. Another sound of water rising from the floor till his sheets floated over his mouth and he woke again and he heard the voices of the women gathered in the square asking to be overtaken by another voice.

Water falls on a landscape emptied of houses and people. Another blight left the earth inhuman. The flood falls to purge the world of any trace but whatever soul speaks through the flood has already forgotten. His body holds to the vision until it fades to fever. And the hills have yet to darken under the drowning sky. Trees drift with their shadows down the ridge where mist still rises.

Those who survived the war for god were returned to earth without a name to remember them. Their swords piled in the square as alms of forgiveness. Years of christening and marriage and death carved in the blades. Runes to mark the fallen. Yesterday was Whitsuntide and the awoken voices drained into pleading that filled the passages of the city. A word he remembers slips through the parade of tongues. A scarred face turns from the wall. Scarred hands lift to fall unclasped.

Each color disappears unless reclaimed by water. And each vision kills you unless reclaimed by hand. The page shrivels weightlessly until he pours water down the crease. Coal shards doused with thumb so the void breaking the horizon unfolds with creaturely forms. Cloaked armies or the startled heads of beasts.

A man who remembers his dreams may bade ghosts pass and the man who forgets them remains haunted. Witness to a world of spectral lines. Colorless and crowded by hollowed faces. Buried eyes. Hands hover in prayer. Smaller creatures also seem to be unperturbed attendants of the flood. A taxonomy for the reawakening.

He awoke smothered by his sheets but another could easily have been aroused by redemption. Images were premised on faith in a world without end. He thought others foolishly believed the opposite. And his hands like those in prayer were severed from the body. Like the blue wing outstretched and the feet of the supplicant apostle that seem to never have walked the earth.

In the towering pillar hovers a gallery of faces with aspects horrifying and serene. Devoured in the maelstrom. On the granite block that confounds the angel with its measurements he had faintly etched a skull. The angel turns from the helplessness forged by his crude counterpart. Bored with the magic he was commanded to learn before the descent heralded by thunder.

The sleeplessness continues whether the vision becomes image or not. The colors seep into the page and he awaits the call to battlements and the raising of the bridge. The faithful answer prophecy with blood. He unrolls the page and sees that he painted the spires of a village beneath the ridge. Not red trees rising from the mist. The alleys have awoken while the flood commences under the guise of dawn and mist cuts through the ridge and unfurls against the waves.

Lee Tyler Williams

Cain's Coat

Harroe was a poor soul. Could never abandon his ghost. He wore a mighty coat of stiffened flesh drenched in ammonia. When anyone asked him where he got it he'd say it was skinned from the mouth of paradise, robbed of Eve's womb, traded for an adze and wobbling mare by Cain himself, settled as a sharecropper after his millennial flight in the backwoods of Tennessee. But never a word of its ignominious origin was to be repeated for rumors beget their own curse. It had more pockets than a torturer's vestment and myriad strings to unveil passages within the viscera lining. In vestibules his sons foregathered all cloaked in rotten cloth with lapels stitched from whore tongues deeply stained with whiskey and soot. By rainfall they relished the dark like opium slaves and their garments shriveled along the hems that sheathed their boots, splitting where they sat and crumbling where they stood. Some coats they stole from clerks and gentlemen pacing courtyards where vigils had vanished with heathen's grace and the fog robed their victims as stealthily as they were stripped. One son nursed a vengeful spleen. Said it had swollen with rain. His liver beleaguered by a soul of its own. He twisted his waxen mustache tips and cursed the frozen hearth. Another read auguries in cockroach husks and charged two copper bits for a discourse on belly ciphers or the positioning of limbs and demanded more drink unless the storms pardoned their crossing. Harroe's sons were all born of various women. Harroe's women all died birthing his sons who never unbuttoned their coats for fear the draft would seep. Before they killed him he had the opening of his coat seamed by a Cantonese tailor's bite and wore it in bed atop the sheets with his holster slung from the coatrack. After they nudged through the bloated fiends plowed in the shavings of the hall and opened the door to his room his youngest shot for the head but the grease lathed on Harroe's coat shimmered and tilted his aim. The gut shot bled damnably like the hemorrhoid of an accountant hunched over the good book and spelling the blessings of blindness. Once the coat was slashed from the corpse most of it spilled through their hands and they carried the dregs behind the saloon to let the wind's scorn reclaim them.

Laurelyn Whitt

Event Horizon

> *Every black hole contains a new universe.*
> —Nikodem Poplawski, theoretical physicist

At the center of the River of Stars
whirling above us   is the end
the edge of the world we have

waited for, believed in   skittering
at the rim of a black hole   an absence
that eats the stars   a different horizon

absolute, relentless.

What lies within it will never escape
or reach us   the earthbound;
what crosses over from our side

never returns.   There
because the mind imagines it to
make sense of the rest

the phenomenal world,
what we perceive or fail to

such as what happens beyond that
one-way portal   past the point

of no return?

or what would there be if we
despite the magnitude of our
brevity   perhaps because

of it   slipped through the fierce
grasp of our galaxy's spiraling
arms   and tumbled over that

dark threshold?

Laurelyn Whitt

Lake Bonneville

Mountains are disappearing
along the Wasatch Front. Their
serrated edges grow

dull, slopes sag, bits of boulder
tumble into talus. Each spring
they melt and avalanche

settling back onto beaches
where an immense lake once
lapped, companionably.

Increasingly it is the lake they remember.

The valley is not a valley;
it no longer cradles the squalling
warmth of bodies.

It is a lakebed whose pluvial
waters rose and fell for millennia
before climbing the slopes,

that brush of shoreline
releasing histories of
orogeny

when the mountains first sprang up
and shook themselves, free of earth
        rearing, raking, rupturing the sky.

Now the lake is all they remember, or care to.

How they rimmed the Great Basin
to contain it; how they suddenly
let it go. How a world so long

in the making

simply vanishes.

Laurelyn Whitt

All Alone Stone†

> *I still look for them. Even though I know they're gone.*
> —Bill Montevecchio

It was as if a song abruptly failed
or was severed:

in that moment, something
in the hummingworld

closed,
fell still.

Listening for an absence
that kept expanding

a sostenuto of stone.

*

If you come for their Feathers
do not give yourself the trouble

of killing them, but lay hold of one
and pluck the best.

You then turn the poor bird adrift,
skin half naked and torn off,

to perish at his leisure.

*

The last Great Auk,
its feathers soft cerements,

stands stuffed & alone
on a solitary herm;

Auk prints surround it.

The moon is crescenting them out.

*

They walked slowly. Jon's bird
went into a corner

but mine was going
to the edge of a cliff.

I took him by the neck
and he flapped his wings.

He made no cry.
I strangled him.

*

There was granite
in the eyes

of the last pair—already
they were petrifying—

as their killer smashed
their egg under his boot.

*

Only the hummingworld
will remember:

how the kite of another
species, loosed

goes soaring

jostling with others
in the darkening skies;

how we begin then
to speak into shadows

as the horizon contracts,

blinks out.

† Passages in italics are drawn from *The Great Auk* by Errol Fuller.

Meg Eden

Ekphrasis on Gulliver's Kingdom Ruins

The stone mermaid on Mount Fuji calls
for the man who cannot answer her—
She calls for the boys in the suicide woods
to come home, for the girls with sarin gas
threats to rest, for her own creator to return
and pluck her confiscated body from demolition.
But can her horn be heard beyond the rotting
fish, suspended on clay strings? When the bull-
dozer rampage is finished, her arms are lifted
in fragments so small that one piece cannot
be discerned from the other, so smooth
their workmanship that her initial presence
will not be marked or remembered.

Laura Hartenberger

Neanderthal Baby

Winning the lottery isn't really relevant to this story, but I want to mention it because since I won, everything that's happened to me seems to be characterized by being post-lottery. For instance, pre-lottery, I might have said "everything I've done," instead of "everything that's happened." Post-lottery, the feeling is that things just happen to me. I'm having a hard time thinking of anything I've specifically done since the lottery happened. I've finished school, but that felt more like absorbing (books, lectures, conversations) than doing (to do a conversation sounds like faking it). I've donated money, but just to organizations that happened to cross my path, not because I carry an allegiance to any particular mission or goal—which might be for the best, since I have this habit of down-talking anything that's actually important to me (even here, positing my post-lottery years as if they're equally important somehow to pre-lottery—as if those two periods had enough in common that they could even be compared). My friends have never told me to stop relating everything back to the lottery, but I'm paranoid that at any moment it might come out that for years they've been finding my tendency to do so irritating or unhelpful or a sign of weakness or uncreativity.

Quickly, then, what's useful to know about me with respect to the lottery is that since I won $30 million at age 19, I: (a) haven't had to decide on any one career or commit to any one field, which has led me to (b) feel at times like I'm not contributing to the world, and yet also means that I (c) can distract myself with enough luxuries not to be overly bothered by this feeling.

All this means that I had the flexibility and freedom to respond immediately and without much real deliberation to the ad in my university's alumni magazine: Professor Seeks Adventurous Woman to Birth Neanderthal Baby.

No one would describe me as adventurous (I've never been on a blind date, or done karaoke, for instance), but I suspected (correctly) that despite its headlining placement, this was not the most important qualification one needed to fill this role. The professor was Dr. Lee, a genetic anthropologist who believed he had successfully reproduced the Neanderthal genetic code with DNA samples extracted from fossilized bone. His plan was to insert this artificial DNA into stem cells, and implant those stem cells into a human egg and create an embryo. All he needed was a live woman to sublet her uterus for a few months.

It is said that we have a limited daily decision-making capacity, and most of it gets taken up with small money-related choices. Big decisions can drain your decision-making capacity for days and you'll find just selecting underwear exhausting and impossible until it gets replenished. I didn't find this one to be a difficult decision. Perhaps I had generous stores of decisioning available, not having to worry about money—or, rather, affordability (I have to worry about money, just differently than most people worry about money)—or perhaps it simply fell in line with my post-lottery pattern of things happening to me without a lot of active pushing from my end. I still haven't precisely communicated this post-lottery feeling: it's some very distant cousin of boredom; a kind of floaty surreality where I can understand and relate to my peers but don't share their concerns and challenges; like I'm an actor plunked down in everyone else's reality, but without the glamour that accompanies that image; and there's a sense that my time is worth both more and less than other people's, and that my time moves both faster and slower than theirs, and generally a sense of being out of sync, in neither a positive nor negative way. Anyway, I suppose no one enters into the decision to have a baby with a full understanding of what it means and the consequences of their decision; having a baby, Neanderthal or not, is as incomprehensible a thing as dying. I used to think I'd never be able to have a baby because I'd be stuck forever at the decision phase, analyzing endlessly what it would mean, and so this project, the ease of its commencement, was a relief in that sense.

My last boyfriend said I like to make things difficult for myself. That may be true.

Another thing I've noticed, being a lottery winner: there's an inverse relationship between money and femininity. Extremely rich women are not seen as sexy, nor as domestic or maternal. I've never had an overwhelming desire to have a child, and winning the lottery only increased my ambivalence. This Neanderthal project seemed like a good in-between: a child that was mine but also belonged to science and to the world. No one would hold me accountable for the child being imperfect—it would be the fault of engineering.

"Realize," Dr. Lee told me in our first meeting, "that we're already living in the past—we're seeing the sun as it was 8 minutes ago, and the stars as they were billions of years ago. Bringing Neanderthals into today's society is just part of the natural process of the universe. Besides, we're all made up of the same material at the atomic level."

What are you creating when you have a baby out of your own hand-me-down DNA? Aren't we all historical artifacts?

Dr. Lee never questioned my motivations, thankfully—I wouldn't have been able to explain it to him. Nor did he seem particularly grateful for my participation, even though I knew he had no other viable candidates. For this, I was glad: I did not want to be treated like a human Petri dish. The best way to describe it would be that he treated me like a colleague, acknowledging that I had my own interests and obligations, and acting as if this were simply one project we were collaborating on.

The process itself was less invasive than a pap smear. Dr. Lee played an astronomy podcast about the shape of the universe. Apparently it's either infinite, or it wraps around itself like a taquito. Through the window I could see an ultimate Frisbee game happening outside on the quad. Overall, it was more pleasant than some pedicures I've had. I realized I hadn't felt this good in a long time, and then the feeling faded and I returned to my standard post-lottery dissociative numb-bliss.

My last boyfriend once said, when my period was late, that he was pretty sure I'd just know if I were pregnant—that something would feel different. This made me very angry, maybe in part because the idea had occurred to me before, too. It was both a relief and a disappointment to discover that nothing felt different about pregnancy—at first, anyway. And then, when things started to shift around and bulge, and my balance went wonky and my sense of smell intensified, and I was being transformed gradually enough that it felt natural but quickly enough that I had trouble recognizing myself when I passed by a mirror—all of this was truly bizarre and inhuman and just extremely weird, but not any weirder than being pregnant with a regular human brand of baby.

One friend asked me, "Don't you want your baby to be smart?" Intelligence hadn't occurred to me, and I was upset for two or three days considering this question. My experience has been that intelligence has very little to do with success or happiness—perhaps in the world of the Neanderthal era it mattered, but in a world where I could be rewarded with $30 million for paying what my friends called the idiot tax, intelligence seemed less than crucial. Besides, the highly regimented scientific impregnation and pregnancy monitoring process seemed to me like a lovely fusion of the stupid and the brilliant: pregnancy, the easiest, most natural thing, engineered with the most sophisticated and sensitive monitoring technologies in existence. Dr. Lee had told me that Neanderthals aren't that different from us, that they might even be smarter. There's evidence, he said, that they used to bury their dead with symbolic tokens. They weren't as unenlightened as we make them out to be.

At five months pregnant, I began to crave meat. At six months, my knuckles and toes began to sprout thick, dark hairs. Dr. Lee had told me about recent studies showing that fetal DNA could migrate into the mother's brain and stay there even after she gave birth. He didn't know if that would happen to me, or if it did, what that would mean.

My mother always said she won the lottery by having me. This used to make me feel good, and then later, at some point, it started to make me feel very sad. My mother's main concern about my pregnancy was that I would become unmarriable. I told her my money had already done that.

If you give away your lottery winnings, you are selfless. If you are a childless woman, you are selfish. If you give your child away, you are mad.

I had one friend who bought lottery tickets several times a week; he felt it was completely unfair that I, a non-regular buyer, could win before him, and he mentioned this to me every time I saw him since. When he found out about my pregnancy, he said, "You didn't feel special enough already?"

The truth is that I don't even remember buying the winning ticket. I found it in my purse with two other losing tickets. I'd had no particular feelings that it was going to work. I didn't recall the mindset I had been in buying it. Buying lottery tickets wasn't a thing that I did regularly—maybe once a year, just enough times that it wasn't a complete once-in-a-lifetime thing, but not often enough to say I earned this win. Lottery buyers seem to both truly believe they are going to win each and every time—while knowing the feeling of losing more intimately that anyone else. If I had really wanted to win, really desired it, I wondered if it would have felt more fulfilling, or more destined.

I get the sense that people want to ask me questions, but they never do. Maybe something about money makes them feel weird asking. With my pregnancy, people asked me lots of questions, mostly variations on "why?" To me, that seems like the most uninteresting question of all—I don't know why anyone but myself would be interested in the answer.

Sometimes I felt, as one of the richest women in the country, like I had reached the endpoint; what was there left for me, or any human, to strive for? Aside from minor annoyances, I had no great conflicts or needs or desires.

Before giving birth, I wrote a new will. For occupation, I wrote "cultural phenomenon." I designated Dr. Lee as Neann's guardian, and, of course, left all my winnings to her. I wondered if her life would be characterized by my winnings post-inheritance. If I died prematurely, I wanted my body to be fossilized, and wrote out instructions for my body to be frozen and then buried in mud in the high arctic tundra, away from predators.

Six months in, I started to feel anxious. If I was unadventurous before, I was a hundred times worse now. I stopped jaywalking. I stopped going outside in the rain. I stopped answering the door. At eight months, the anxiety turned into a desperate need to flee the city. A cave in the middle of the forest sounded nice, or maybe a grassy savannah where I could run barefoot through the grass, chasing down small mammals. I wanted to be alone, without my comforts or the attention. I wanted to simply exist, without any of the complications.

Spending my lottery winnings made me feel like a vessel—I was moving funds into the world in various ways as I lived through the days. Being pregnant didn't feel dissimilar. I was a conduit for the child, for the science experiment, and it was overall enjoyable to participate in the movement of these things forward. "You've brought an entire species back from extinction," they said to describe me at the galas and award ceremonies. "Without you, we'd be in the Dark Ages—or, not in them, as the case may be!" The jokes never ended, and they all told them with the same delight, reveling in their own intelligence, living at such a height of science that it could be joked about.

When it finally arrived, my Neanderthal baby was a barely breathing thing, a mass of strange cells formed into a red, writhing body that looked like I had always suspected my insides to appear. When they told me that it was not, in fact, Neanderthal—it had only human DNA, that there must have been some mistake—they were not as accusatory as they could have been. They even let me keep it—the child that was suddenly completely mine, that was not going to live a life of science. And so I went home to my comfortable lottery winner's house, with my lottery winner's child, and we sat together on the couch and I thought about how I had always liked to make things difficult for myself.

Danielle Sellers

Placing Blame

It's bad luck to keep a conch shell in your house. If you have a daughter, she'll never marry, or if she does, it won't last.
—a Key West superstition

I remember whole glass lamps filled with the tiny things,
embryonic in their spirals. A curtain of shells strung
together like enamel beads separated our kitchen
from the den. A queen conch on the wicker étagère
big and pink as my face, attracting nothing but dust.

In high school, the conch was our mascot. A shell
stood at the entrance, hurricane-cracked, pieced back,
tall as three freshman girls stacked on each other.
Inside, it was hot and damp as a mouth.
We heard the folk tale but never dreamed.

The Florida Kongo people believe the shell is a symbol
for the day's cycle, and life's. When you die, your soul
finds water. I imagine souls sitting knee to knee
in an infinite circle, a game of duck-duck-goose.
Placed on a grave, the shell maps the tagged's way back.

The world is born feathered, slimy, or cocooned,
with egg-teeth or not. Some human mothers
scoff at superstition. They hunt beaches
for the horns that call their daughters to water,
coiled, fat-bellied, always between beginnings.

Danielle Sellers

Lament in Early Summer

Another yellow flapper caught
by the neighbor's wizened tom
this morning. Mid-ascension,
paws slapped together and crushed it
like a bubble between a child's palms.
The surprise of it,
(the bird's, a bubble's),
brief life ending. The bird sensing
it's over. The child and cat
in awe of their own brute strength.
Because I am three states away
he is seeing another woman.
She is willing to give herself over
to his hard and dangerous hands.
How young she must be! And how
terrible it is, to be a bird among cats.
Even after the body is cold,
the cat will take it in his teeth,
toss it up, re-enact the act of killing
until the bird is spent of feathers,
that glorious first desire.
Oh to be something like a bubble,
that doesn't know its purpose
is short-lived, or when the dream
of flight is realized, then dashed—
Terrible to have your heart carried,
even ever so gently, in another's mouth.

Danielle Sellers

For a Body I'm Not Allowed to Touch

He is *l'esclave rebelle*
    chains imagined, chin uplifted,
abdomen lean, the sinews taut.
    Michelangelo mastered his body,
delivered him from stone.
    His muscles swell above the hip bones

transverse from travertine ribs and pelvis,
    His fascia is a warrior's,
 a hoplite greased with sweat
    and the blood of fresh-killed lamb,
the way his tunic might slip down his body.
    His is the corset muscle of a Greek boy's,

a Senator's lover lounging
    on silk pillows, thin linen tunic
barely there. He sips wine. He laughs.
    Hoary men tremble at the display
of his midriff, how the delicate flesh
    dimples with each contraction and release.

Eros moves jeweled hands along it.
    Neither he nor I know its proper name.
It's man's dowry, conquering lovers and slaves.
    I call it Solomon's Throne,
Hector's Spear. Each side its own name.
    Its own history of birth and war.

Danielle Sellers

Matin

Now, finally, I wake without first thoughts of you.
The dogs huff and whine—first canonical sounds
of the day. Then, what to buy at market,
who to write. Used to, I had all morning
to languish in your imagined arms, your chest
against the pearls of my spine. But after so many
years of not touching, the heft of your hand
on my pyramidal breasts and hips,
your breath's hot bouquet, finally elude me.

Douglas Jackson

Cedar Bluff

On Mussel Beach, proof abrades underfoot, wears thin, diminishes with time and touch.

We swam there, in the Clinch, remember? The trees were in young leaf. Branches reached out above us, like the arms of kneeled worshippers called to prayer, caught mid-bow.

Our bodies bobbed in a rapid stretch, then slowed into the fading ripples. It was quieter just beyond the bend, and above the calls of birds, I heard the small splash of your movement. At seventeen you couldn't see it, but you lacked the clumsy discomfort some of us felt in our own skins, a quality in later years I would assign to you as grace.

The first time: you looked at me like you saw me. You moved to the shore, and I followed. The other times—more than a dozen in less than a year—I drew on that first connecting glance, but I can't swear that it was ever repeated.

The year's science topic was *The Role of Biodiversity in Southwest Virginia*. We talked about stewardship. We avoided placing blame. We continued the quiet coexistence of competing pursuits displayed like a physical Appalachian trait. "What's mined is ores," you used to say, playing with words to amuse yourself. It wasn't quite right, because coal isn't an ore, but carbonized plant matter, fossilized life. You rarely took things seriously, and details would have implied a certain gravity.

A detail: Your eyes are the gray-green color of the Rogersville Shale exposed at the Cut. Your parents' genes determined the color. The highway department made the Cut, revealed the ancient rock. It's hundreds and hundreds of millions of years old, pushed upward 250 million years ago in a collision of plates.

In the final project, we wrote of the spill from the tanker truck and its milky kill of 18,000 mussels in a tributary to our very river. We praised our community's part in the recovery efforts, our care for the remaining mussels in Indian Creek. We scripted our feelings: what it felt like to stand knee-deep among something so small, but so precious that it gave our town prominence. We talked of the nursery (putting those mussels to bed, as you said), of protecting habitat and learning to recognize what we saw.

The naming of the endangered—tan riffleshell, purple bean, rough rabbits-foot—are colored with the hope of our human connection. But you maintained an air of fatalism, the sense that—whether they extinguish or prosper—our actions didn't really make a difference.

Reporting in front of the class: "There are at least sixteen different species of mussels in the Clinch River alone," you said. "We need these things. And not just to clean the water—which they do." Your deep voice was stronger than I ever imagined myself to be. More than one girl in the room paid special attention. Your cousin Joe prepared a spitball. "We need things that aren't alike. We need these different species to reproduce to keep our system going."

We were taking turns talking, having practiced our presentation. I was proud, standing there: even if my shoulders weren't as broad or my arms as big, I was friends with Tommy Belcher. The whole class could see.

According to plan, it was my turn to speak, yet you continued: "Not everything is meant to reproduce, or even survive, and maybe some traits doom us to extinction." That line hadn't been there in our report. You added it.

The quiet in the room was a bored silence, but it felt like an accusation. Eyes stared blankly. I flushed with crashing waves of flight and fight instincts. "The weak don't survive." The clock hand moved.

I never asked you about it, though it was clear something had changed. As we stood there, a fog settled around us like the low clouds that pour across the ridge to mask the rounded peaks above the town.

"Already," I said, stumbling into my next memorized part, "about 99 percent of the species that ever existed have gone extinct."

Before school let out that year, you went to the river with me again. We floated. Our limbs touched in the currents as the river spun us, occasionally, accidentally, too infrequently.

I tried not to watch as you stood, or rather, I tried not to let you see me look as you stood among insect drone. You stepped onto that shell-ridden stretch, feet bare as the rest of you, buttocks and thighs displaying the mechanics that allowed you to absorb the jagged barbs of the beach underfoot. You didn't flinch, but moved to the bank, and like an explorer leaving the jungle, you stepped through that stand of pawpaws, with their tropical looking leaves and hard green beginnings of fruit. This time you didn't wait for me.

We had found our way together, interdependent, intertwined on at least one stretch of the river, then a quiet summer passed in a seemingly endless string of late afternoon storms. I spent a good deal of time watching the hall phone, willing it to ring. Every time I passed the built-in shelves by the front door, I touched the collections that Momma had built there over the years, I rubbed the heads of ceramic angels, pressed the tip of my index finger against the horn points of unicorns. The plastic dinosaurs that J. D. had added from his toy chest seemed less lucky, but occasionally I rubbed a back or two before heading out in hopes of catching sight of you, of you pulling your F-150 up to the sidewalk where I walked, telling me to get in the truck. In everything I did, you lurked somewhere in my thoughts.

From the bridge, I saw a couple of field biologists working in the river. They counted mussels in silos, confirming growth measured against some standard.

I went back to pick the pawpaws once school started back, but either the raccoons or you had gotten to them first.

Cindy Rinne

Reflections

Words spoken by green
skeleton
dwelling at the base

of the Giant Fig
echo through
his thin rib spaces.

Flamingo, Masai
giraffe, and
impala listen

drinking from alka-
line, shallow
Lake Manyara. I

was fishing in a
boat and see
a mermaid-like figure.

I watch her again
on the water's
edge. Mami Wata

combs curly, black hair,
peers in the
mirror. Her large snake

wraps around her, safe.
Mami flees
to the lake leaving

behind gems and watches.
Good fortune!
I am a rich man.

Watermama comes
as a dream
demands her jewels

returned. Her terms:
Agree to
be faithful and I

stay wealthy. Refuse
and become
ill, dying in this

tree cave, her shrine.
Bells, candles,
statuary, yams,

palm wine, and my skull—
sacrificed,
an earthly death

under frayed, red
cloth banner
and fig blossom hiss.

Cindy Rinne

Ancestors Dance

Eagle migrated to the lands of the Ice Tribe.

Diffused patches of light sparkled on his wings.

Among the greenish glow of the northern lights

Native ancestors danced in the next life.

Sealskin boots stomped and turned on a floor lit by stars.

Eagle thanked the sky for this gift of colors.

Asked the Sitka Spruce if he could gather pine needles.

They will be wrapped around the joints

Of the feather ladder.

The pine scent made him dizzy.

He ceased motion. Perched on the rough skin.

I will give my spiky needles to you. First, listen to the story
Of what is below my raised roots. The history of the Tree Tribe had its
Origins when the frozen land was warm. Our language was born
Of earthquakes; growing our roots deep.

Eagle stretched and saw evidence below the tree's roots

Of duckbilled and polar dinosaurs who endured

Months of cold and dark.

Then wooly mammoths caught in permafrost.

The cave lion of rounded ears, tufted tails, and tiger-like stripes.

Layers of migratory caribou with fur and a dense undercoat.

Thanked the spruce for its needles and the history of ice told by bones.

Zeke Jarvis

What Happened to the World's Sweetest Jukebox?

Years ago, when America was still largely an industrial-based economy, there was a real need for a place that would serve boilermakers at 8 in the morning. Milwaukee, Wisconsin, had a particularly good place for that, which makes sense, if you know much about the city. In addition to being a home of many breweries (for those not in the know, a boilermaker is a beer with a shot of whiskey in it), Milwaukee had a strong base of manufacturing for a long time. It still does, I suppose. When I was driving a visiting poet up to the university, we came over the Hoan Bridge, we saw some smokestacks, and he said, "Well, there's a nice view." I started to explain to him that not all of Milwaukee looks like that, but he stopped me to tell me that this was, to him, a symbol of America's economic strength. It meant that here was a city with jobs, a city with a sense of life and vibrancy. This was a New York poet (and a neurotic one, no less) telling me this, which was cool. That's what this essay is about, I suppose: the weird connection between unlikely folks.

But, for the moment, let's get back to boilermakers. This bar I was talking about was called the National Avenue Liquor Bar. It's a pretty functional title. It was a bar that served liquor and was located on National Avenue. I say "was" located, because it was replaced by a Walgreen's a few years ago. Fucking figures. But the pragmatism of the name probably appealed to its core demographic. The point of the bar wasn't to be stylish or even vaguely appealing. The point was to have cheap drinks with familiar faces. I assume they served mixed drinks, but the raison d'etre of the National Avenue Liquor Bar (you heard me) was beer and shots. The patrons of this bar drank to get drunk, and, thanks to their modest goals, they usually succeeded. That's admirable to me.

I can verify the success of their efforts, because a couple of months before the bar closed down, a friend and I headed there so that we could bare witness to this place before it shut its doors forever. As we entered, a blend of flannel-wearing old factory workers and scrawny ne'er-do-wells regarded us. We were both wearing jeans and t-shirts, which made us fit in for the most part, but we were both much too young to pass for regulars. Still, we headed to the bar and looked at our options. Icehouse was on tap for 90 cents a glass (a small glass, I might add), and it seemed like an appropriate option. I think the 90-cent price was to allow for dime tips for our bartender, a pudgy woman wearing a black tank top and black spandex shorts, who told us that, if she was out of the bar, we should just holler for her. Although we were in graduate school, we figured that we were less broke than she was, so we left her dollar tips, I think, though it seems strange now that we'd leave tips bigger than our drink costs. We also felt sympathetic for her, because she showed us the names of her children, whch were tattooed in a heart on her chest. She seemed nice, though she also had the gruffness that any female bartender in a place like the National Avenue Liquor Bar would have to have.

So, we bellied up to the bar with our 90-cent beers and watched the television, as seemed to be the custom. The man to the right of me was also watching intently and, every few minutes, would raise his fist in the air, well above his head, for no discernible reason. But, as my friend and I sat and drank and talked, we started to realize something about the jukebox. It only had two genres of music, and they didn't generally go together. About two thirds of the songs were old country, which came as no surprise to either of us. But the remaining third was Motown. We chuckled a bit as we discussed this, but it started to make sense. It was the standard music for black and white working class of a certain generation. There was something sweet about the idea of a shithole bar in Milwaukee (a place one of my professors during my undergrad work at UW-Madison had told me was the most segregated city in the country) being a place that united people on the basis of class rather than splitting them on the basis of race. Even if it required a social lubricant, there was something appealing about that.

Of course, there's theory, and there's practice. In practice, a bar that lets you carry out Mad Dog 20/20 is bound to have some fighting in it. But that's part of its charm. The night we were there was a relatively mild (partially because we left before midnight, I'm sure) argument, but before I get to that, let me describe another patron at the bar that night. Just to the right of the fist raiser, a middle-aged woman had plopped down and, leaning around the fist raiser, struck up an intermittent conversation with me. She'd begun by asking me, "Are you a cop?"

I assured her that I wasn't. She insisted that I looked like a cop, and she would ask me multiple times if I was, then if my father was, then if I had a brother who was a cop. The other strand of the conversation she initiated with me, which I tried to escape by talking with my friend (though I suspect he was sometimes letting our conversation lag so he could watch this woman talk to me more), was to tell me, "You're so handsome ...you look just like my son." Oedipal proclivities aside, this observation wasn't welcome, because I could tell this woman had some sort of mental disability, though what it would have been specifically was outside of my area of diagnostic ability. Nevertheless, she consistently asked me if I was a cop and told me that I was good-looking (like her son).

This brings me back to the fighting. As we drank, towards the other end of the bar, a shouting match was gradually building. My friend's memory is that it revolved around the jumble in the newspaper (you know, the puzzle on the comics page where you have to rearrange letters to form an actual word), and this may well have been true, but I found myself too rattled by the vaguely incestual desires of this bedraggled woman sitting on the other side of the fist raiser to really pay attention. In any event, as the shouting match took on a greater level of both urgency and volume, the woman looked at me and told me, "I don't like the way they're talking to each other. If you're a cop, then you should do something." At that point, I was a little buzzed and growing tired of her attention, so I raised my hands in defense and said, "I'm not a cop, I don't have any authority here." To this, the woman smiled and told me, "Oh, you've got authority."

My friend found this incredibly entertaining. So do I, in retrospect, but at that moment, the attention of the woman and the vague threat of the fist raiser's unpredictability left me frazzled and defeated. I think it was shortly after that exchange that we left for another establishment. I wouldn't say that the trip wasn't worth it by any stretch of the imagination. It was outstanding. Easily preferable to a night of uneventful martini drinking at an upscale bar or about five nights of recklessness at some overpriced club. What made it so terrific was character. Both the characters in the bar and the character of the bar. What other place would offer disturbingly good deals and the atmosphere of a beer-soaked pack of cigarettes. It's sort of like listening to the Dead Milkmen: those who get it love it, but if someone doesn't connect to it, it's impossible to explain the appeal to them.

But like the good, church-going kid who dies in a car accident, the National Avenue Liquor Bar couldn't possibly continue to exist in this awful world. Its demise was tragically predictable. That comparison might seem unfair, even offensive, but let's consider it for a moment. This was a place designed to please the customer. It served cheap drinks to working folks. It didn't care about race or style or whether you had a reason to put your fist up in the air while you watch TV. But shouldn't that have been enough? Isn't gentrification, if that's what putting a Walgreen's in can be called, putting a bandage on a neighborhood (thereby covering not only its wounds but its culture as well) instead of helping the people in the neighborhood? But, to be honest, I don't really wonder where the people who frequented the bar went. There are plenty of bars in that neighborhood. But I do wonder what happened to that jukebox. That symbol of cross-cultural drinking. It chills me to think that it might have ended up in a dump somewhere. After all, who would take it? The owner? If so, what are the chances the music on it is actually enjoyed? Certainly not by crowds. The main problem of homogenization could be that there just aren't any surprises anymore. Predictability can, sadly, obliterate an interest in the traditional expressions of one's own culture. In the melting pot, how can that jukebox stand firm? I'm well aware of the problematic nature of this defense. This isn't a beautiful union of all mankind. Sure, Johnny Cash was a drunk, Willie Nelson was a pothead (still is, I hope), and the Jackson 5 were, well, the Jackson 5. But isn't that exactly who should be speaking for and to this crowd? I'll go ahead and say that I'd rather listen to the Highwaymen than some shitty muzak that came out of Taylor Swift. Even if I have to have a mentally deficient drunk hit on me to do it. Especially if that's the case, come to think of it.

Darren Stein

All That Remains

I look at the remains of the Abrahams' lives—
Two octogenarians now carted off to the home:
he, to the hospital section, near to certain death;
she, to pine away, alone among strangers, waiting
for the ever diminishing weekend visits from her
children and other family members.

No one has bothered with a garage sale—
What was of value, the family has taken—the rest
lies strewn across the pavement outside their building
for backpackers and ravens to pick through the remains;
a warped book shelf; an old mattress; pretty, stained
coasters from some holiday they took in the sixties—
the detritus of a marriage, an independent little world,
now piled onto a heap at the side of the road for the
garbage men to drag away and dump along with the
rest of life's refuse.

Freya Sachs

Closure

The envelope factory is empty,
abandoned on Chicago's river bank.
How much spit this saves, the licking—
questions of content:

mysteries, inquiries, bills,
the little things: correspondence
to be closed before
it finds a home.

Sealing is an art: of wax, water,
bits of our bodies:
how strange, to lick,
to enclose words
with parts of our
selves.

Notes on Contributors

Elmaz Abinader is author of a memoir, *Children of the Roojme: A Family's Journey from Lebanon* (University of Wisconsin Press, 1997), and a poetry collection, *In the Country of My Dreams* (Sufi Warrior Pub, 1999). Winner of a Goldies in Literature, a PEN Oakland/Josephine Miles Award, she has been a Fulbright Scholar and a recipient of the Oregon Drammies for "Country of Origin," a one-woman play. She teaches at Mills College in Oakland, California, and is co-founder of VONA/Voices. Her recent poetry collection, *This House, My Bones,* is forthcoming from Willow Press in September 2014.

Majnun Ben-David was an anthropologist in Africa until he returned to the United States and decided that fiction was a better way to tell the truth. He can be found online at majnunbd.com, @majnunbd, or majnunbd@gmail.com

Lauren Camp is the author of *This Business of Wisdom* (West End Press, 2011) and a brand new collection, *The Dailiness* (Edwin E. Smith Pub, 2013). She was a juror for the 2014 Neustadt International Prize for Literature and guest editor for special sections in *World Literature Today* (on international jazz poetry) and *Malpaís Review* (on the poetry of Iraq). Her writing is forthcoming in *Brilliant Corners, The Portland Review, Sweet, About Place,* and *Feminist Studies.* Lauren has been a radio producer and host on Santa Fe Public Radio since 2003. More information can be found at www.laurencamp.com

Jennifer Clark's first book of poems, *Necessary Clearings,* is set to be released this summer by Shabda Press. Her work has appeared in *Failbetter, Main Street Rag, Midwest Quarterly, Structo,* and *Fiction Fix,* among others. She lives in Kalamazoo, Michigan.

Rebecca Clever graduated from Chatham University in 2011 with an MFA in creative writing. She has served as a contributing reporter, community newspaper editor, columnist, promotional and technical writer, and managing book editor and designer. Her work has appeared in various newspapers, literary journals, and anthologies. She is the first recipient of the Laurie Mansell Reich Poetry Award co-sponsored by the Academy of American Poets and Chatham University, was a quarter-finalist for the 2012 Nimrod Literary Awards Pablo Neruda Prize for Poetry, and is a past nominee for the AWP Intro Journals Project.

Susan Cohen is the author of *Throat Singing* (WordTech, 2012). Her work has appeared in *Greensboro Review, Prairie Schooner, River Styx, Southern Humanities Review*, and *Southern Poetry Review*, among others. Her honors include the Anderbo Poetry Prize, Literal Latte Poetry Award, and Rita Dove Poetry Award. She lives in Berkeley, California, and earned an MFA from Pacific University.

Meg Eden, whose work has been published in various magazines, has been nominated for a Pushcart Prize and received the 2012 Henrietta Spiegel Creative Writing Award. She was a reader for *The Delmarva Review*. Her collections include *Your Son* (The Florence Kahn Memorial Award, NFSPS, 2012) and *Rotary Phones and Facebook* (Dancing Girl Press, 2012). Check out her work at: http://artemisagain.wordpress.com/

Frances Gapper is the author of *The Tiny Key* (Sylph Editions, 2009) and *Absent Kisses* (Diva Books, 2002). She has work in *Short Fiction* (University of Plymouth Press) and *The Moth*, an Ireland-based journal.

Damyanti Ghosh is a freelance writer for nonfiction magazines and journals. Her short fiction has been published in *Birkbeck Writer's Hub, Quarterly Literary Review Singapore, Muse India*, and in print anthologies by Marshall Cavendish Singapore, Monsoon Books Singapore, and MPH publications Malaysia. She is working on her first novel.

John Gosslee's work appears in *Yale Review, Quiddity, Gargoyle, Mudfish,* and *Bitter Oleander*. He is the editor of *Fjords Review,* and his latest testament is blitz-krieghq.com

Laura Hartenberger's writing has been published in *CutBank Magazine, Dragnet, Nano Fiction, Winter Tangerine Review*, and others. She has won prizes from *Gulf Coast Magazine* and *Hart House Review*.

Parul Kapur Hinzen earned an MFA from Columbia University. Her articles and reviews have appeared in *The New Yorker, Newsday, The Wall Street Journal Europe, The American Book Review, The Atlanta Journal-Constitution*, and *ARTNews*. She has written short fiction for *Frank* (Paris), *Wascana Review, Allegheny Review,* and *Amherst Review*. Her first novel, *Inside the Mirror*, was short-listed for the 2013 Horatio Nelson Fiction Prize. She is a book critic with ArtsATL.com, Atlanta's leading online arts review.

Daniel Hudon is originally from Canada and is now an adjunct lecturer in math, physics, astronomy, and writing in Boston. He is writing a book on extinct species to raise awareness about the present biodiversity crisis. Parts of the book appear in *Canary*, *Toad*, and *The Chattahoochee Review*.

Douglas Jackson lives and writes in Roanoke, Virginia. He has received the Tennessee Writers Alliance Short Fiction Award, the James Andrew Purdy Award for Fiction, and the Bay to Ocean Fiction Award. His stories appear in *Haunted Voices, Haunting Places: An Anthology of Writers of the Old and New South*, *The Delmarva Review*, and *Clay Bird Review*. Douglas is a graduate of Duke University; the University of California, Irvine; and the creative writing program at Hollins University. He works with the Virginia Department of Housing and Community Development.

Zeke Jarvis is an associate professor at Eureka College. His work has appeared in *Bitter Oleander*, *KNOCK*, and *Petrichor Machine*, among others. His first book, *So Anyway . . .*, is forthcoming from Robocup Press in 2014.

Amanda Larson is a writer and artist on Whidbey Island, Washington. When she isn't writing or drawing, she is growing and propagating heirloom plant varieties. She has a particular interest in biodiversity and the preservation of traditional ways of life.

Christina Lovin is the author of *Echo* (Bottom Dog Press, 2014), *A Stirring in the Dark* (Old Seventy Creek Press, 2012), and the Finishing Line Press chapbooks *Flesh* (2013), *Little Fires* (2008), and *What We Burned for Warmth* (2006). Lovin's writing has appeared in numerous journals and anthologies. The Society for Humanistic Anthropology chose her heroic crown sonnet, "Myth Information," recipient of the 2009 Ethnographic Poetry Award. The Southern Women Writers' Conference awarded Lovin the 2007 Emerging Poet Award. She has been a finalist for the Rita Dove International Poetry Award, has received the Judson Jerome Scholarship from Antioch Writers' Workshop and the Baron Wormser Scholarship for Stone Coast Writers' Conference, and was awarded the 2008 AWP WC&C Poetry Scholarship. She is currently a lecturer in the English and Theatre Department at Eastern Kentucky University.

Mark McKain's work has appeared in *The New Republic*, *AGNI*, *The Journal*, *American Letters & Commentary*, *Green Mountains Review*, and elsewhere. He has an MFA from the University of Florida and teaches screenwriting at Full Sail University.

Sarah Fawn Montgomery holds an MFA in creative nonfiction from California State University, Fresno, where she was an editorial assistant for *The Normal School*. She is a PhD candidate at the University of Nebraska-Lincoln and serves as the senior nonfiction reader for *Prairie Schooner*. Her essays have been listed as notable in *Best American Essays* and her poetry and prose have appeared or are forthcoming in various journals including *Crab Orchard Review*, *DIAGRAM*, *Fugue*, *Georgetown Review*, *The Los Angeles Review*, *North Dakota Quarterly*, *Puerto del Sol*, and *The Pinch*, among others.

Elizabeth Deanna Morris has a BA in creative writing from Susquehanna University. She is currently pursuing her MFA at George Mason University. Her work has appeared or is forthcoming in *Whiskey Island*, *OVS*, and *Hotel Metal Bridge*. Her chapbook, *Patterning*, is forthcoming from Corgi Snorkel Press in the summer of 2014.

Travis Mossotti teaches creative writing at Lindenwood University, and his poetry has appeared in *Antioch Review*, *Denver Quarterly*, *Michigan Quarterly Review*, *Prairie Schooner*, *Poetry Ireland Review*, *Southwest Review*, *The Southern Review*, *The Writer's Almanac*, *Western Humanities Review*, among others. Mossotti was awarded the 2011 May Swenson Poetry Award by contest judge Garrison Keillor for his first collection of poems, *About the Dead* (Utah State University Press, 2011), and in 2010 his poem "Decampment" was adapted to screen as an animated short film. The Sustainable Arts Foundation awarded Mossotti a grant in 2012 in support of a working collection of poems entitled *Field Study*, and he was also named Poet-in-Residence at the Endangered Wolf Center in St. Louis, Missouri. He is the author of the chapbook *My Life as an Island* (Moon City Press, 2013).

Ezra Olson is a senior English major in writing at Northwestern University. He was awarded four honors by Northwestern University's English department: best poem (for "Selections"), best short story, a second-place award for a critical essay—and the title of best junior creative writing major. He was selected as one of three Daniel Bonbright Scholars, a distinction awarded to outstanding humanities students.

Lynn Pedersen's work has appeared in *New England Review*, *The Comstock Review*, *Poet Lore*, *Southern Poetry Review*, *The Palo Alto Review*, and *Cider Press Review*. She is the author of *Theories of Rain* (Main Street Rag, 2009), a poetry chapbook. A graduate of the Vermont College of Fine Arts, she lives in Atlanta, Georgia.

Cindy Rinne creates art and writes in San Bernardino, California, and is a guest author for Saint Julian Press. She is a founding member of PoetrIE, an Inland Empire based literary community. Her work appeared or is forthcoming in *The Lake*, *Revolution House*, *Soundings Review*, *East Jasmine Review*, *The Gap Toothed Madness*, *A Narrow Fellow*, *Poetry Quarterly*, *The Prose-Poem Project*, *Tin Cannon*, and *The Wild Lemon Project Literary Journal*. She has a poetry manuscript, "The Feather Ladder," and has written a chapbook titled *Rootlessness*. www.fiberverse.com.

Matt Rotman's poetry and short stories have been featured in *Diabolique Magazine*, *Aberration Labyrinth*, and Illinois State University's literary journal, *Euphemism*. His screenplay, "Casa Infierno," was made into an independent film in 2006. He currently lives in San Diego, California, where he is working on the first draft of the Great American Gothic Horror Novel. He is the founding editor of *Crooked/Shift*.

Freya Sachs received an MFA in creative writing at Vanderbilt University in 2008. She teaches high school English and environmental science in Nashville, Tennessee.

Susan Sailer completed an MFA in poetry at New England College in 2007. Her poems have appeared in such journals as *THEMA*, *Poetry East*, *Platte Valley Review*, and *5 A.M.* She has published a chapbook, *Coal* (Finishing Line Press, 2012), and a full book, *Ship of Light* (Port Yonder Press, 2013). Sailer lives in Morgantown, West Virginia. Her reviews have appeared in *Indiana Review*, *Prairie Schooner*, and *Kestrel*.

Danielle Sellers has an MA from The Writing Seminars at Johns Hopkins University and an MFA from the University of Mississippi, where she held the Grisham Poetry Fellowship. Her poems have appeared or are forthcoming in *River Styx*, *Subtropics*, *Smartish Pace*, *Cimarron Review*, *Poet Lore*, *Prairie Schooner*, *32*

Poems, and elsewhere. She is the author of *Bone Key Elegies* (Main Street Rag, 2009). In 2011 she was awarded a Walter E. Dakin Poetry Fellowship to attend the Sewanee Writers' Conference. She edits *The Country Dog Review* and lives in Winter Springs, Florida.

Mary Senger is an English education student at Illinois State University. She enjoys writing and is currently producing her first short film, "Hoffman Heights."

M.E. Silverman is the editor and founder of *Blue Lyra Review* and review editor of *The Museum of Americana*. His poems have appeared in *Crab Orchard Review*, *32 Poems*, *Chicago Quarterly Review*, *The Southern Poetry Anthology*, *The Los Angeles Review*, *Mizmor L'David Anthology: The Shoah* (Poetica Magazine, 2010), *Cloudbank*, *Neon*, *Many Mountains Moving*, *Pacific Review*, *Sugar House Review*, among others. He was a finalist for the 2008 New Letters Poetry Award, the 2008 De Novo Contest, and the 2009 Naugatuck River Review Contest. His recent publications are the chapbook *The Breath Before Birds Fly* (ELJ Press, 2013) and *The Bloomsbury Anthology of Contemporary Jewish American Poetry* (Bloomsbury Academica, 2013), co-authored with Deborah Ager.

Judith Skillman's new collections are *Broken Lines—The Art & Craft of Poetry* (Lummox Press, 2013) and *The Phoenix: New and Selected Poems 2007–2013* (Dream Horse Press, 2013). Her poems have appeared in *Poetry*, *Prairie Schooner*, *FIELD*, *The Midwest Quarterly*, *The Iowa Review*, *The Southern Review*, *A Cadence of Hooves*, among other journals and anthologies. She is the recipient of grants from the Academy of American Poets, the Washington State Arts Commission, the Centrum Foundation, and the King County Arts Commission. She teaches for Yellow Wood Academy. More information at judithskillman.com

Darren Stein is an Australian artist, teacher, and poet. Born in Johannesburg, South Africa, in 1973, he worked in the townships and squatter camps around Johannesburg and Soweto during the transition to democracy in the early 1990s. His community work included adult education, post-apartheid reconciliation, and police reform. After suffering from post-traumatic stress disorder caused by his exposure to the violence of the period, he immigrated to Sydney, Australia. He now teaches history and comparative religion at a college on Sydney's North Shore. His poems have appeared in various anthologies, including *Over the Rainbow* (1996), *The Liquid Mirror* (International Library of

Poetry, 1998), *An Endless Place* (International Library of Poetry, 1999), *Storage Space: A collection of contemporary poetry* (Xlibris Corps, 2008), and *Poetica* (2013).

Ursula Villarreal-Moura earned her MFA from Sarah Lawrence College. She was the winner of the 2012 *CutBank* Big Fish Flash Fiction/Prose Poetry Contest. Her writing has appeared in *CutBank, Emerson Review, The Doctor T.J. Eckleburg Review, Lunch Ticket, Vol. 1 Brooklyn, NAP*, and elsewhere. She tweets about books @Ursulaofthebook

J. Weintraub has published a variety of fiction, essays, poetry, and transla-tions in all sorts of literary reviews and periodicals, including *The Massachusetts Review, Modern Philology, Gastronomica,* and *Prairie Schooner.* Many of his pieces have been anthologized, and he is a recipient of Illinois Arts Council Awards for fiction and creative nonfiction. He has been an Around-the-Coyote poet, a StoneSong poet, and has had one-act plays produced by the Theatre-Studio in New York City, the Summer Place Theatre in Naperville, Illinois, and Theatre One in Middleboro, Massachusetts. He is currently a network playwright at Chicago Dramatists.

Lenore Weiss lives in Sterlington, Louisiana, and completed an MA in cre-ative writing at San Francisco State University. Her work has been published in *San Francisco Peace and Hope, The Portland Review, Poetica Magazine, The Más Tequila Review, Digital Americana, The Journal of Feminist Studies in Religion, Nimrod International, Copper Nickel,* and *Bridges: A Jewish Feminist Journal.* Her collections include *Cutting Down the Last Tree on Easter Island* (West End Press, 2012) and *Two Places,* forthcoming from Kelsay Books. Lenore serves as the copy editor for *Blue Lyra Review.* Her blog resides at www.lenoreweiss.com.

Laurelyn Whitt's poems have appeared in various North American journals, including *Nimrod International, The Tampa Review, Puerto Del Sol, The Malahat Re-view, PRISM International, Rattle, Descant,* and *The Fiddlehead.* She is the author of three award-winning poetry collections, including *Interstices* (Logan House Press, 2006). *Tether* (Seraphim Editions, 2013) is her latest collection. She lives in Minnedosa, Manitoba.

Lee Tyler Williams was born in Irving, Texas. He lives in Louisiana and works as a housepainter and freelance copywriter. His work can be found in *absent magazine, thieves jargon,* and at National Public Radio, among other places.

www.ingramcontent.com/pod-product-compliance
Lightning Source LLC
Chambersburg PA
CBHW051304250626
47155CB00009B/3431